Lanzo's words were beguiling. Her eyes flew open. It was good to see him.

During the last grim months of her marriage and her subsequent divorce, Gina had felt as though she were trapped in a long dark tunnel. But the unexpectedness of seeing Lanzo again made her feel as though the sun had emerged from behind a storm cloud and was warming her with its golden rays.

Her blue eyes clashed with his glinting gaze. She did not want to talk, she admitted shakily. She was so aware of him that her skin prickled. Perhaps he really was a magician and could read her mind, because his eyes narrowed and—to her shock and undeniable excitement—he slowly lowered his head.

"Lanzo…?" Her heart was thudding so hard she was sure he must hear it.

"Cara," he murmured silkily. He had wanted to kiss her all evening. Even though she had carefully avoided him for most of the party, his eyes had followed her around the room and he had found himself recalling with vivid clarity how soft her mouth had felt beneath his ten years ago. Now the sexual tension between them was so intense that the air seemed to quiver. Desire flared, white-hot, inside him, and his instincts told him that she felt the same burning awareness. Anticipation made his hand a little unsteady as he lifted it to smooth her hair back from her face.

All about the author...
Chantelle Shaw

CHANTELLE SHAW lives on the Kent coast, five minutes from the sea, and does much of her thinking about the characters in her books while walking on the beach. An avid reader from an early age, she found that school friends used to hide their books when she visited, but Chantelle would retreat into her own world, and she still writes stories in her head all the time.

Chantelle has been blissfully married to her own tall, dark and very patient hero for more than twenty years and has six children. She began to read Harlequin romance novels as a teenager, and throughout the years of being a stay-at-home mum to her brood, she found romance fiction helped her to stay sane! Her aim is to write books that provide an element of escapism, fun and of course romance for the countless women who juggle work and a home life and who need their precious moments of "me" time. She enjoys reading and writing about strong-willed, feisty women and even stronger-willed sexy heroes.

Chantelle is at her happiest when writing. She is particularly inspired while cooking dinner, which unfortunately results in a lot of culinary disasters! She also loves gardening, taking her very badly behaved terrier for walks and eating chocolate (followed by more walking—at least the dog is slim!).

Chantelle Shaw

THE ULTIMATE RISK

TORONTO NEW YORK LONDON
AMSTERDAM PARIS SYDNEY HAMBURG
STOCKHOLM ATHENS TOKYO MILAN MADRID
PRAGUE WARSAW BUDAPEST AUCKLAND

Recycling programs
for this product may
not exist in your area.

ISBN-13: 978-0-373-13004-7

THE ULTIMATE RISK

First North American Publication 2011

Copyright © 2011 by Chantelle Shaw

www.Harlequin.com

Printed in U.S.A.

THE ULTIMATE RISK

CHAPTER ONE

Did every woman remember her first lover? Gina wondered.

Surely she was not the only woman to have felt her heart slam against her ribs when she had glanced across a crowded room and caught sight of the man she had once been madly in love with?

It was definitely Lanzo. Their brief affair had taken place ten years ago, but he was regarded as one of Europe's most sought-after bachelors. Photographs of him regularly featured in celebrity gossip magazines and he was instantly recognisable. She couldn't help staring at him, conscious of that same swooping sensation in the pit of her stomach that she had felt when she had been eighteen and utterly in awe of him.

Perhaps he felt her scrutiny? Her breath caught in her throat when he turned his head in her direction. For a few seconds their eyes met and held, before Gina quickly looked away and pretended to idly scan the other guests at the party.

The tranquillity of Poole Harbour, on England's south coast, had been shattered over the weekend by the staging of the international offshore powerboat racing championships. Generally regarded as the most extreme and dangerous of all watersports, powerboat racing had been going on all day far out in the bay. But this evening the engines were silent, and dozens of sleek, futuristic-looking powerboats were moored in the harbour, bobbing gently on the swell.

It was certainly a sport that attracted the beautiful people, Gina noted, as she glanced around the restaurant where the after-race party was being held. Glamorous promotional models—uniformly tanned, blonde, and sporting unnaturally large breasts and very short skirts—flocked around bronzed, over-loud male boat crews, the drivers and throttle-men, who between them sent their boats skimming over the waves at death-defying speeds.

She had never understood why anyone would choose to risk their life for fun, and she had taken no interest in the racing. The party was definitely not her scene, and she had only come because her old schoolfriend Alex had recently taken over as manager of the exclusive Di Cosimo restaurant, and had requested her moral support on his first big event.

Instead, it was she who was in need of support, Gina reflected ruefully. Her legs felt like jelly and her head was spinning—but she could not blame either on the one glass of champagne she had drunk.

She was so shocked to see Lanzo again. She hadn't realised he was still involved in powerboat racing, and it had not crossed her mind that he might attend the party. True, he owned the restaurant, but it was one of many around the world belonging to the Di Cosimo chain, and she had not expected Lanzo to be in Poole. She was unprepared for her reaction to him, for the way her stomach muscles clenched and the tiny hairs on her arms prickled when she studied his achingly familiar profile.

With his striking looks—olive-gold skin, classically sculpted features, and silky jet-black hair that showed no signs of grey, even though he must be in his mid-thirties by now—Lanzo di Cosimo looked like one of those impossibly handsome male models who featured in fashion magazines. Tall and powerfully built, his tailored black trousers emphasised his height, and his white shirt was of such fine silk that the hard ridges of his abdominal muscles and the shadow of his dark chest hairs were visible beneath the material.

But it was more than just looks, Gina thought, as she stared down at her empty glass and dragged oxygen into her lungs. Lanzo possessed a simmering sensual magnetism that demanded attention. Supremely self-assured and devastatingly sexy, he was impossible to ignore, and the women who thronged around him made no attempt to hide their fascination with him.

He was a billionaire playboy whose passion for dangerous sports matched his passion for leggy blondes—none of whom remained in his life for long before he exchanged them for another model. Ten years ago, Gina had never really understood what he had seen in her—an averagely attractive brunette. But at eighteen she had been too overwhelmed by his interest to question it, and only later had realised that her attraction had probably been her embarrassingly puppy-like eagerness. Lanzo had not had to try very hard to persuade her into his bed, she acknowledged ruefully. For him she had been a convenient bedmate that summer he had spent in Poole, and no doubt he hadn't meant to break her heart—she only had herself to blame for that.

But time and maturity had healed the wounds of first love, she reminded herself. She was no longer the rather naïve girl with a massive crush on him she had been a decade ago. Resisting the urge to glance over at Lanzo again, she turned her back on him and strolled over to the huge wall of windows that ran the length of the restaurant and offered wonderful views over the harbour.

* * *

Lanzo shifted his position slightly so that he could continue to watch the woman in the blue dress who had caught his attention. He recognised her, but to his frustration could not place her. Now that she had her back to him he saw that her gleaming brown hair fell almost to her waist, and he imagined threading his fingers through the silky mass. Perhaps he had noticed her because she was so different from the blonde groupies who always attended the after-race parties, he mused, feeling a flicker of irritation when the young woman at his side, sensing that he was distracted, moved closer and deliberately pressed her nubile body up against him.

The girl *was* young, he thought with a frown as he glanced at her face, which would be far prettier without the thick layer of make-up. In her thigh-high skirt and ridiculous heels she reminded him of a baby giraffe—all gangly legs and long eyelashes. He doubted she was much over eighteen, but the invitation in her eyes told him he could bed her if he chose to. Once he would have been tempted, he acknowledged. But he was no longer a testosterone-fuelled twenty-year-old; his tastes had become more selective over the years, and he had no interest in girls barely out of high school.

'Congratulations on winning the race,' the blonde said breathlessly. 'I think powerboat racing is so exciting. How fast do you go?'

Lanzo stifled his impatience. 'The boat can reach a top speed of one hundred miles an hour.'

'Wow!' She smiled at him guilelessly. 'I'd love to go for a ride some time.'

He winced at the idea of giving 'rides' in his pride and joy. *The Falcon* was a million pounds' worth of superlative marine engineering. 'Racing boats are not ideal for sightseeing trips because they are built for speed rather than passenger comfort,' he explained. 'You would have more fun on a cruiser. I'll speak to a friend of mine and see if he'll take you on a trip along the coast,' he murmured, as he gently but firmly prised the girl's hand from his arm and moved away from her.

Gina watched the setting sun cast golden rays across the sea and gild the tops of the trees over on Brownsea Island. It was good to be home, she mused. She had spent most of the last ten years living and working in London, and she had forgotten how peaceful it was here on the coast.

But thinking about home, and more specifically her new, ultra-modern flat with its sea views, a little way along the quay, filled her with anxiety rather than pleasure. Since she had lost her job with a local company she had been unable to keep up with the mortgage repayments. The situation was horribly similar to the time when she had struggled to pay the mortgage and bills on the house she and Simon had owned in London, after he had lost his job and she had become the only wage earner.

After she had left him the house had been sold, but because it had been in negative equity she had come away with nothing. She had no savings—hence the reason why she had taken out such a large mortgage to buy the flat. But now it looked increasingly as though her only option was to sell her new home before the bank repossessed it.

Her life wasn't turning out the way she had planned it, she thought dismally. She had always assumed that a few years spent building her career would be followed by marriage and two children—a boy and a girl called Matthew and Charlotte. Well, she'd had the career, and she'd had the marriage, but she had learned that babies didn't arrive to order, however much you wanted them, and that marriages didn't always last, however hard you tried to make them work.

Her hand strayed unconsciously to the long, thin scar that ran down her cheek close to her ear, and continued down her neck, and she gave a little shiver. She had never expected that at twenty-eight she would be divorced, unemployed and seemingly infertile—the last evoked a familiar hollow ache inside her. Her grand life-plan had fallen apart, and now the prospect of losing the flat that she had bought when she had moved back to Poole, in the hope of starting a new life away from the bitter memories of her failed marriage, was the final straw.

Lost in her thoughts, she jumped when a voice sounded close to her ear.

'How do you think it's going?' Alex asked tensely. 'Do you think there's enough choice of canapés? I asked the chef to prepare twelve different types, including three vegetarian options.'

'It's a great party,' Gina assured him, pushing her concerns to the back of her mind and smiling at Alex. 'Stop looking so worried. You're too young for grey hairs.'

Alex gave a rueful laugh. 'I reckon I've gained a few since I took over as manager here. Lanzo di Cosimo demands the highest standards at all his restaurants, and it's important that I impress him tonight.'

'Well, I think you've done a brilliant job. Everything is great and the guests seem perfectly happy.' Gina paused, and then said in a carefully casual tone, 'I didn't realise that the head of Di Cosimo Holdings would be here.'

'Oh, yeah. Lanzo visits Poole two or three times a year. If you had come home more often instead of living it up in London, you would probably have seen him around,' Alex teased. 'He comes mainly for the powerboat racing, and a

year or so ago he bought a fabulous house on Sandbanks.'
He grinned. 'It's amazing to think that a little strip of sand
in Dorset is one of the most expensive places in the world to
live.' He suddenly stiffened. 'Speaking of the devil—here
he comes now,' he muttered below his breath.

Glancing over Alex's shoulder, Gina felt her stomach
lurch when she saw Lanzo striding in their direction. It
didn't matter how firmly she reminded herself that she was
a mature adult now, and well and truly over him. Her heart
was pounding and she felt as awkward and self-conscious
as she had been when she'd had a summer job as a waitress
in this very restaurant ten years ago.

His eyes were hypnotic—perhaps because their colour
was so unexpected, she thought shakily, her gaze drawn
against her will to his face. With his swarthy complexion
and jet-black hair, brown eyes would have seemed more
likely, but his irises were a startling vivid green, fringed
with thick black lashes and set beneath heavy brows.

Time had done the impossible and improved on perfection, Gina decided. At twenty-five, Lanzo had been a
sleek, incredibly handsome man who had still retained a
boyish air. A decade later he was rugged, sexy, and utterly gorgeous—his face all angles and planes, his slashing
cheekbones and square jaw softened by a mouth that was
full-lipped and blatantly sensual.

Something stirred inside her—something that went
deeper than sexual attraction. Although her physical reaction to him *was* shockingly intense, she acknowledged,
flushing when she saw Lanzo lower his gaze to the outline
of her nipples, clearly visible beneath her dress.

A long time ago he had held her in his arms and she had
felt certain that he was the only man in the world for her.
So many things had happened since then. She had escaped
from a violent marriage and knew that she was strong and

could look after herself. But for a crazy moment she wished Lanzo would draw her close against his broad chest and make her feel safe and *cherished*, as he had made her feel all those years ago.

But of course Lanzo had never really cherished her, she reminded herself sharply. It had just been an illusion—part of a silly daydream that he would fall in love with her as she had fallen in love with him. And, like most daydreams, it had turned to dust.

'The party is superb, Alex.' Lanzo greeted his restaurant manager, his eyes still focused on the woman at Alex's side. 'The food is excellent—as people expect from a Di Cosimo restaurant, of course.'

Alex visibly relaxed. 'Thank you. I'm glad you approve.' He suddenly realised that he did not have Lanzo's full attention, and gestured to Gina. 'Allow me to introduce a good friend of mine—Ginevra Bailey.'

'Ginevra—an Italian name,' Lanzo observed softly. He was intrigued by her obvious reluctance to shake his hand, and the slight tremble of her fingers when she placed them in his palm. Her skin was soft and pale, in stark contrast to his deep tan, and he had a sudden erotic image of her naked—of milky-white limbs entwined with his darker ones. He lifted her hand to his mouth and grazed his lips across her knuckles, feeling an unexpectedly sharp tug of desire in his gut when her eyes widened and darkened.

Gina snatched her hand from Lanzo's grasp, feeling as though an electrical current had shot along her arm. She swallowed and struggled for composure. 'My grandmother was Italian, and I was given her name,' she murmured coolly, thankful that the years she had spent working for the very demanding chairman of a world-renowned department store chain meant that she was an expert at hiding her private thoughts. Hopefully no one would guess that

Lanzo's close proximity was making her heart race so fast that she felt breathless and churned up inside.

His green eyes glittered and she quickly looked away from him, assuring herself that he could not possibly read her mind. He gave a small frown as he studied her intently. She sensed that he was intrigued by her, but she had no intention of reminding him that they had once, very briefly, been lovers. Ten years was a long time, and undoubtedly countless other women had shared his bed since her. It was far better, and less embarrassing, that he did not recognise her. And, to be fair, it was not his fault that, while she had not forgotten him, he had presumably never given her a second thought after he had casually announced at the end of that summer a decade ago that he was returning to his home in Italy.

Lanzo's eyes narrowed as he studied Ginevra Bailey. Something about her tugged on his mind, but the faint memory was elusive. And as he skimmed his gaze over her hourglass figure, displayed to perfection by a navy blue silk-jersey dress that clung to her curves, he was certain that if they *had* met on a previous occasion he would not have forgotten her.

Her beauty was understated: a perfect oval-shaped face, skin as smooth as porcelain, and deep blue eyes that were almost the exact shade of her dress. Once again something stirred in his subconscious—a distant recollection of eyes as intensely blue as the deep ocean—but the memory remained frustratingly intangible, and perhaps it was nothing. He had known many women, he acknowledged wryly. It was possible that Ginevra Bailey simply reminded him of a past mistress whose identity eluded him.

Beside him, Alex made a slight movement, and Lanzo realised with a jolt that he was staring at the beautiful brunette. He resisted the temptation to reach out and run his fingers through the long chestnut-brown hair that rippled down her back and inhaled sharply, his body taut with sexual anticipation. He had not been so instantly turned on for a long time, and his reaction was all the more surprising because he was usually attracted to tall, willowy blondes. The woman in front of him was a delectable package of voluptuous curves who was having a profound affect on his libido, and Lanzo was in no doubt that he intended to bed her at the first opportunity.

'I hope you are enjoying the party, Ginevra,' he murmured. 'Are you a fan of powerboat racing?'

'No. I've never seen the attraction of dangerous sports,' Gina replied shortly.

She was struggling to disguise her overwhelming awareness of Lanzo, and must have sounded more abrupt than she had intended because Alex interspersed quickly, 'Gina was responsible for the floral displays tonight. The table centrepieces are beautiful, don't you think?'

'Indeed.' Lanzo glanced at the arrangement of red and white roses and trailing variegated ivy on a nearby table. 'You are a florist then...Gina?' He frowned, wondering why the shortened version of her name seemed familiar.

'Not professionally. It's simply a hobby,' she replied. During her marriage to Simon he had encouraged her to take an expensive flower-arranging course, as well as an even more expensive course of lessons in French cuisine, so that she could be the perfect hostess at his business dinner parties. The cookery lessons were not of much use now that she was only preparing meals for herself—often a ready-meal heated up in the microwave, Gina thought ruefully—but she had enjoyed making the floral displays for the party.

'The floristry firm I'd originally booked were forced to pull out because of staff illness,' Alex explained. 'Luckily

Gina offered to step in and decorate the tables.' He paused as he caught sight of one of the waiters frantically signalling to him from across the room. 'There seems to be some sort of crisis in the kitchen,' he muttered. 'Would you excuse me?'

Gina watched Alex thread his way through the throng of guests, feeling a flutter of tension now that she was alone with Lanzo. Of course they were not really alone, she reminded herself impatiently. The restaurant was packed with party guests, but as she slowly turned back to him she felt the strangest sensation that they were in a bubble, distanced somehow from the hum of voices around them.

Surely every woman remembered her first lover? she told herself again. Her response to Lanzo was a natural reaction to seeing a face from the past. But deep down she knew it was more than that. She'd had a couple of relationships before she had married, but no other man—not even Simon in the happier times of their marriage—had evoked this helpless, out-of-control longing; this violent, almost primitive desire that shocked her with its intensity.

Lanzo had been incredibly special to her, she acknowledged. Although their affair had not lasted long, the discovery that a man like him—an international jet-set playboy who could have any woman he wanted—had desired her, had boosted her confidence. Because of him she had changed from a shy teenager into a self-assured woman who had built a successful career and later caught the eye of an equally successful City banker.

But if Lanzo had given her confidence Simon had stripped it from her, she thought ruefully. Thanks to her disastrous marriage she no longer had faith in her judgement of others. She felt stupid that she had not realised what Simon was really like beneath his charming exterior, and right now she was wary of Lanzo's potent masculinity and felt painfully vulnerable.

To her relief a waiter approached and offered to refill her glass. Usually she only had one drink at social events—a throwback to all the times Simon had drunk too much at parties and become embarrassingly loud and unpleasant. But tonight she was grateful for any distraction from Lanzo's overwhelming presence, and when the waiter had gone and she was alone with him once more she took a hurried sip of her champagne and felt the bubbles explode on her tongue.

'So you don't like powerboat racing?' he drawled, in his gravelly, sexy accent. 'Are there any forms of watersports you *do* like?'

'I enjoyed learning to sail in the bay when I was a child. Sailing is rather more peaceful than tearing through the water at a ridiculous speed,' she said pointedly.

'But not as adrenalin-pumping,' Lanzo murmured, his eyes glinting with amusement when she blushed.

Gina had a horrible feeling that he knew her adrenalin levels were sky-high as her instincts sensed the threat he posed to her peace of mind and she prepared to fight him or flee.

'Do you live locally, Gina?' The way he curled his tongue around her name caused needle-darts of pleasure to shiver across her skin.

'Yes, I was born here. Actually, I'm the fourth generation of Baileys to be born in Poole—but the last, I'm afraid, because I don't have any brothers to carry on the family name.' She knew she was babbling but it was preferable to an awkward silence, when Lanzo might hear the loud thudding of her heart. She took a deep breath and prayed that her usual calm nature would reassert itself. 'Are you staying in Poole for long, Signor di Cosimo?'

'Lanzo,' he corrected her. 'Regrettably, this is only a short trip as I have other business commitments, but I hope to return soon.' He studied her flushed face and smiled. 'Perhaps sooner than I had planned,' he drawled.

Gina felt trapped by a powerful force that would not allow her to tear her eyes from Lanzo's face. They were alone in a room full of people, bound together by a powerful chemistry that held them both in its thrall.

Lanzo watched her pupils widen until her eyes were deep, dark pools, and his body tautened as heat surged through his veins. She had intrigued him from the moment he had glanced across the room and discovered her watching him. It happened to him all the time. Women had stared at him since he was a teenager. But never before had he felt such a strong urge to respond to the desire that darkened her eyes to the colour of midnight.

The loud smash of glass shattering on the tiled floor hurtled Gina back to reality, and she looked around to see that one of the waitresses had dropped a tray of glasses. She was shocked to realise how close she was standing to Lanzo and she jerked back from him, her face burning when she caught the hard gleam in his eyes. How long had she been staring at him like an over-awed teenager? she wondered, feeling hot with embarrassment. She had no recollection of either of them moving, but their bodies had been so close that her pelvis had almost brushed against his.

Tearing her gaze from him, she saw that the waitress was trying to gather up the shards of glass with her hands. 'I'll get a broom,' she muttered, and hurried across the restaurant, grateful for the chance to escape Lanzo's intent stare.

He watched her walk away from him, feeling himself harden as he studied the gentle sway of her bottom beneath its covering of tight navy silk.

Oh, Gina! What a transformation time had wrought, he mused, for he had suddenly solved the puzzle of why she seemed familiar. He remembered her now—although she looked very different from the shy waitress who had followed him around with puppy-dog devotion and been so sweetly anxious to please him that summer he had spent in England.

He had not known that her proper name was Ginevra. It suited the sophisticated woman she had become. And really it was not surprising that he had initially failed to recognise her, he assured himself, because this elegant woman, with her toned figure and her mane of glossy chestnut hair, bore scant resemblance to the slightly plump, awkward girl who had delighted him with her unexpectedly passionate nature when she had been his lover for a few weeks one summer, a long time ago.

Was the grown-up Gina still the sensual, uniquely generous lover who had appeared in his dreams for several months after he had returned to Italy? Lanzo brooded. Events in his life had taught him to live for the present and never revisit the past. But he was prepared to make an exception in this instance, he mused, watching her until she disappeared into the kitchens with a determined gleam in his eyes that would have worried her had she seen it.

CHAPTER TWO

IT STILL wasn't completely dark, even though it was almost eleven o'clock, Gina noted when she emerged from the restaurant and glanced up at the indigo sky which was studded with a few faint stars. The water in the harbour was flat and calm, and the salt tang carried on the breeze was a welcome contrast to the stifling atmosphere of the restaurant.

She loved the long days and balmy evenings of June, and she paused for a moment, enjoying the fresh air which was cool but did not require her to slip on her jacket, before she turned and began to stroll along the quay.

'I did not realise that you still lived in Poole.' A tall figure stepped out of the shadows, and Gina's heart skittered when Lanzo fell in step beside her. 'I visit several times a year and I'm surprised I haven't seen you around.'

Gina gave him a startled glance, her heart thudding with the realisation that he had finally recognised her. The expression in his eyes made her pulse quicken. It was the intense, predatory look of a panther stalking its prey, she thought, and then gave herself a mental shake. He was just a man, she reminded herself irritably. But the soft night air carried the spicy drift of his aftershave, and as her senses quivered she ruefully acknowledged that Lanzo would never be 'just' anything.

'Perhaps you did see me on one of your previous visits, but you didn't remember me,' she said tartly, still feeling faintly chagrined that he had not realised her identity back at the restaurant.

'Oh, I remember you, Gina,' he said softly. 'Although I admit I did not immediately recognise you tonight. You've changed a lot since I knew you.'

He wanted to run his fingers through her long silky hair, but he had noticed how she had tensed the moment she had seen him outside the restaurant. The flash of awareness in her deep blue eyes when she had first spotted him had told him that she was as conscious of the fierce sexual chemistry between them as he, but for some reason she seemed determined to ignore it.

'Your hair especially is different from the style you wore ten years ago,' he commented.

'Don't remind me,' Gina groaned, utterly mortified by the memory of the curly perm she had believed would make her look older and more sophisticated than the ponytail she'd had since she was six. The perm had been a disaster, which had transformed her hair into an untameable bush with the texture of wire wool, and rather than looking sexy and sophisticated she had resembled a chubby poodle. As if the perm hadn't been bad enough, she had been a few pounds overweight, she remembered grimly. 'I can't imagine why you ever noticed me,' she muttered.

In all honesty he had *not* taken much notice of her when he had first arrived in Poole to oversee the launch of the Di Cosimo restaurant here all those years ago, Lanzo remembered. Gina had simply been one of the staff—a part-time waitress who helped out with the washing up on nights when the restaurant was especially busy.

She had been a shy, mousy girl, with an annoying habit of looking at the floor whenever he spoke to her—until on one occasion he had been so irritated by her studious inspection of the carpet that he had cupped her chin in his hand and tilted her face upwards and had found himself staring into the bluest eyes he had ever seen.

The unremarkable waitress was not so ordinary after all, he had been amazed to discover, as he had studied her flawless peaches-and-cream complexion and her wide, surprisingly kissable mouth. He could not remember their conversation—it had probably been something inconsequential, like asking her to fill the salt-cellars—but after that he had noticed her more often, and had invariably found her watching him. Although she had blushed scarlet and hastily looked away whenever he had met her gaze.

That summer ten years ago had been a dark period in his life, Lanzo reflected grimly. Alfredo had died in the spring, and he had been struggling to come to terms with the loss of the man he had regarded as a second father—the man who would have been his father-in-law had it not been for the devastating fire that had swept through the di Cosimo family home and taken the lives of Lanzo's parents and his fiancée five years before that.

Cristina's face was a distant memory now—like a slightly out of focus photograph—and the pain of her loss no longer felt like a knife being thrust through his heart. But he remembered her; he would always remember the gentle girl he had fallen in love with all those years ago.

Widower Alfredo and Lanzo's parents had been delighted when he had announced that Cristina had agreed to be his wife. But a week before the wedding tragedy had struck.

The familiar feeling of guilt made Lanzo's gut clench, and he stared out across the harbour to where the darkening sky met the sea, lost in black memories. He should not have gone on that business trip to Sweden. Cristina had begged him not to, saying that they needed to talk. But he had been shocked by her revelation that she was pregnant—so unprepared for the prospect of having a child when they had both decided that they would wait at least five years before they started a family.

He had been so young—only twenty—and determined to make his father proud of him as he took on more responsibilities at Di Cosimo Holdings. But that was no excuse, he thought grimly. He'd known Cristina had been hurt by his lack of enthusiasm for the baby. He hadn't wanted to talk about it, and instead had insisted on going on the business trip when he had known full well that he could have sent one of his staff in his place. But he had wanted time alone, to get his head around the idea of being a father, and so he had ignored Cristina's tears and flown to Sweden.

Within twenty-four hours he had realised that he had behaved like an idiot. He loved Cristina, and of course he would love their child. He had been impatient to get home and convince her that he was delighted about the baby, but his meeting had overrun, meaning that he had missed his flight, and he'd had to spend another night away. The following morning he had arrived in Italy and been met by Alfredo, who had broken the devastating news that his parents and Cristina had all died in the fire that had destroyed the di Cosimo villa.

Lanzo's jaw tightened as he remembered the agony of that moment—the feeling that his heart had been ripped from his chest. He had not told Alfredo that Cristina had been a few weeks pregnant. The older man had been utterly distraught at the loss of his only daughter and there had seemed little point in making his grief worse. But the bitter truth was that he could not bear anyone to know how he had failed his fiancée and his unborn child, Lanzo acknowledged. He should never have gone away. Cristina had died believing that he did not want their child, and he had never been able to forgive himself for not being with her when she had needed him most.

Alfredo had never got over losing his daughter, but the older man had become an invaluable father figure and advisor, for with his own father gone Lanzo had become the head of Di Cosimo Holdings at the age of twenty. Five years later Alfredo's death had hit him hard, but he had dealt with it as he had dealt with the loss of Cristina and his parents—by burying his grief deep in his heart.

The opening of a new restaurant in England had given him an excuse to spend some time away from Italy and his memories. He had thrown himself into work, and into off-shore powerboat racing, which was a popular sport along the south coast. It had satisfied a need in him to push himself to his limits and beyond. He'd loved the speed, the danger and the adrenalin rush, the idea that death was one flip of the boat away—for deep down he had not really cared what happened to him. Subconsciously he had hoped that one day he would push himself too far and death would take him, as it had Cristina. But for fifteen years he had cheated death and been left alone to bear his grief. Sometimes he wondered if it was his punishment for those first doubts he'd had about being a father.

'I noticed you,' he told Gina abruptly. She had been a calming influence on his crazy mood that summer—a nondescript girl with a gentle smile that had soothed his troubled soul.

For the first two years after Cristina's death he had not looked at another woman, and when he had finally started dating again his relationships had been meaningless sexual encounters. He had closed the door on his emotions and deliberately chosen mistresses who accepted his terms. But Gina had been different. Something about her youthful enthusiasm had reminded him of the carefree days of his own youth—a time that seemed bathed in perpetual sunshine before the black cloak of grief had settled on his shoulders. When he'd been with Gina his mood had lightened, and he had enjoyed spending time with her. It had only been when he had found himself thinking about asking her to return to Italy with him that he had realised there was a danger she was starting to mean something to him—and he had immediately ended their affair. For he associated love with pain, and he never wanted to experience either emotion ever again.

'You were sweet and shy, and you used to stare at me when you thought I didn't notice,' he said gruffly. She had seemed painfully innocent, although she had assured him that she'd had several boyfriends, Lanzo recalled.

Sweet was such an unflattering description. It conjured an image of a silly lovesick teenager—which of course was exactly what she had been ten years ago, Gina thought ruefully. She remembered how her heart had thudded with excitement whenever Lanzo had been around—rather like it was doing now, a little voice in her head taunted. But the difference now was that she was a confident career woman—albeit one without a career at the moment—and she was perfectly in control of her emotions.

'I admit I had an outsize crush on you,' she said lightly. 'But it was hardly surprising when I'd attended an all-girls school and had little contact with the male species—especially the exotic Italian variety.'

'Why didn't you remind me tonight that we knew each other?' Lanzo asked her curiously.

She shrugged. 'Because it was a long time ago, and I barely remembered you.'

His mocking smile told her he knew she was lying, and she was thankful that it was probably too dark now for

him to notice her blush. They had reached the attractive
block of six flats on the quayside where she lived, and as
she slowed her steps he halted in front of her.

'But you did not forget me completely during the past ten
years,' he stated arrogantly, his deep, velvety voice sending
a little quiver down Gina's spine. 'Are you cold?' he asked,
noticing the tremor that ran through her.

'Yes,' she lied again, 'but I live here. Well,' she said
briskly, desperate to get away from him before she made
a complete idiot of herself, 'it's been nice to meet you
again.'

She stepped back from him, but instead of bidding her
goodnight he smiled and moved closer, so that they were
enclosed in the shadowed porch area in front of the flats.

'You can't have lived here long. These flats were
still under construction when I was here last year,' he
commented.

'I moved here from London four months ago.'

'That must have been a big change,' Lanzo murmured,
glancing over his shoulder at the fishing boats moored in
the harbour.

Gina nodded. 'I worked in the City and I'd forgotten
how quiet it is here.'

'What job do you do? I assume you have moved on
from waiting tables?' he said, his eyes glinting as he
allowed them to roam over her navy silk dress and matching stiletto-heeled sandals. It was impossible to equate this
elegant woman with the curly-haired young waitress from
ten year ago.

'Until recently I was PA to the chairman of the Meyers
chain of department stores.'

He looked impressed. 'That's certainly a long way from
waitressing. Meyers have outlets in virtually every major

city around the world. But surely you don't commute to the City from here every day?'

'No, I decided to leave the company when my boss retired. There were a number of reasons why I wanted to move out of London.' Not least the late-night abusive phone calls from her ex-husband, Gina thought grimly. 'My father suffered a heart attack at Christmas. He's recovered well, thankfully, but I decided to move closer to my family. Dad's illness brought it home to me that you never know what the future holds.'

'Very true,' Lanzo said in a curiously flat tone. Gina gave him a curious glance, but his expression was unfathomable. 'Too often we take the people we care about for granted.'

She nodded. 'I came back to Poole to work as the PA for the head of a construction company. Unfortunately the market for new houses has been hit by the recession, and Hartman Homes went into liquidation last month. I've been looking for a new job, but there's not a lot around. The way things are going I might need to take up waitressing again,' she quipped, trying to quell the familiar flare of panic that thoughts of her precarious finances induced.

'Come and see me at the restaurant in the morning. I may be able to help you,' Lanzo murmured.

She gave him a startled glance. 'I was joking about being a waitress,' she told him, privately thinking that she would consider almost any job in order to keep up with her mortgage repayments.

'I'm serious. I urgently need a personal assistant to fill in for my usual PA while she is on maternity leave. Luisa had planned to work up until her baby was born, but she has high blood pressure and has been advised to give up work early. Her absence is causing me all sorts of problems,'

Lanzo added, sounding distinctly unsympathetic for his secretary.

'High blood pressure can be dangerous for an expect-ant mother and her unborn child,' Gina told him. 'I'm not surprised your PA has been told to take things easy. She couldn't have travelled with you in the later stages of her pregnancy anyway. Pregnant women shouldn't fly after about thirty-six weeks.'

'Shouldn't they?' Lanzo shrugged. 'I admit I know little about pregnancy—it is not something that interests me.' He had never come to terms with his belief that he had failed his unborn baby, and he had vowed never to have another child. 'But you seem very knowledgeable on the subject.' He frowned as a thought struck him. 'Do you have a child?'

'No,' she said shortly. Since she had moved back to Poole she had met several of her old schoolfriends, pushing prams around the town, and invariably the question of whether she had children had cropped up. The answer always hurt, Gina acknowledged, however much she laughed and made the excuse that she had been too busy with her career, and there was plenty of time for babies.

'Some of my friends and both my stepsisters have chil-dren, so obviously I've picked up a few facts about preg-nancy. I hope your PA keeps well in the final weeks before her baby is born,' she murmured, feeling a sharp pang of sadness that every woman but her, it seemed, had no prob-lem conceiving a child.

That wasn't true, she reminded herself. Endometriosis was a well-known cause of female infertility, although for years she hadn't realised that her heavy and painful periods were an indication of a medical condition that could affect her chances of having a baby.

Her gynaecologist had explained that there were various

treatments available that might help her conceive, but he had emphasised that to maximise her chances she should try to fall pregnant before she reached her thirties. As a recently divorced twenty-eight-year-old, she had been forced to face the heartbreaking fact that she might never be a mother, Gina acknowledged bleakly.

'Where have you gone?'

Lanzo's voice tugged her from her thoughts and she stared at him helplessly. Seeing him tonight had taken her back in time. Life had been so optimistic and so full of exciting possibilities when she had been eighteen, but the last few years especially had been chequered with disappointments, she thought sadly.

That summer she had spent with Lanzo was a golden memory she had treasured, and even the misery she had felt after he had returned to Italy had served a purpose. Desperate to put him out of her mind, she had decided to move away from Poole, where it had seemed that every street and quaint country pub held memories of the few weeks they had spent together, and instead of accepting a place at nearby Bournemouth University she had taken a secretarial course, moved to London, and forged a highly successful career.

But Lanzo had been right when he had guessed that she had never forgotten him. Oh, she'd got over him—after a while. She had grown up and moved on, and he had faded to the background of her new, busy life. But occasionally she had found herself thinking about him, and curiously it had been Lanzo, not Simon, she had dreamed about on the night before her wedding. Now, unbelievably, he was here, watching her with an intense expression in his mesmeric green eyes that made her heart-rate quicken.

'I...I really must go in,' she said faintly.

His slow smile stole her breath. 'Why?'

'Well…' She searched her blank mind for a good reason. 'It's getting late. I should get to bed…' She cringed. Why had she used *that* word? She had been fighting her memories of his toned, tanned, naked body—of his hands gently pushing her thighs apart so that he could sink between them. She felt the hot throb of desire low in her pelvis and closed her eyes, as if blotting him from her vision would free her from his sorcery.

'Stay and talk to me for a while,' he said softly. 'It's good to see you again, Gina.'

His words were beguiling. Her eyes flew open. It was good to see him too, she acknowledged silently. During the last grim months of her marriage and her subsequent divorce she had felt as though she were trapped in a long dark tunnel. But the unexpectedness of seeing Lanzo again made her feel as though the sun had emerged from behind a storm cloud and was warming her with its golden rays.

Her blue eyes clashed with his glinting gaze. She did not want to talk, she admitted shakily. She was so aware of him that her skin prickled, and her nipples felt as hard as pebbles, straining against the constriction of her bra. Perhaps he really was a magician and could read her mind. Because his eyes had narrowed, and to her shock and undeniable excitement he slowly lowered his head.

'Lanzo…?' Her heart was thudding so hard she was sure he must hear it.

'Cara,' he murmured silkily. He had wanted to kiss her all evening. Even though she had carefully avoided him for the rest of the party after she had gone to report the broken glass to the restaurant manager, his eyes had followed her around the room and he had found himself recalling with vivid clarity how soft her mouth had felt beneath his ten years ago. Now the sexual tension between them was so intense that the air seemed to quiver. Desire flared, white-

hot, inside him, and his instincts told him that she felt the same burning awareness. Anticipation made his hand a little unsteady as he lifted it to smooth her hair back from her face.

Gina stiffened at Lanzo's touch and instinctively jerked her head back. She had concealed her scar with make-up, but she was mortified to think that he might feel the distinct ridge that ran down her cheek and neck.

'Don't.' The plea left her lips before she could stop it. She flushed when his brows rose quizzically. He had every right to look surprised, she thought miserably. Seconds ago she had been leaning close to him, waiting to feel the first brush of his mouth over hers. But when he had touched her face she had been catapulted from her dream-like state back to reality.

She could not bear to see the desire in his eyes turn to revulsion—as would surely happen if he saw her scar. Even worse would be his curiosity. What if he asked her how she had been injured? Nothing would induce her to make the humiliating admission that her ex-husband was responsible for the unsightly scar that now served as a physical reminder of her gullibility.

It sickened her to think that once she had believed she loved Simon, and that he loved her. Only after their wedding had she realised that she had not known the true nature of the man, who had hidden his unpredictable temper beneath a charming façade. She felt ashamed that she had been taken in by Simon, and had sworn that she would never be so trusting again. What did she really know of Lanzo? her brain questioned. Her heart had leapt in recognition when she had first seen him tonight, and all evening she had been swamped with memories of their affair, but in truth her relationship with him ten years ago had lasted for a matter of weeks and he was virtually a stranger.

Lanzo's eyes narrowed as he watched Gina physically and mentally withdraw from him, and for a few seconds a mixture of anger and frustration flared inside him. She had wanted him to kiss her. He knew he had not imagined the desire that had darkened her eyes to sapphire pools. So why had she pulled back?

The young Gina of his memories had been open and honest, and she had responded to him with an eagerness that he had found curiously touching. It appeared that the more mature, sophisticated Gina had learned to play the games that so many women played, he thought grimly. He had had mistresses in the past who had calculated his wealth and made it clear that their sexual favours came at a price: jewellery, designer clothes, perhaps being set up in a luxury apartment. He presumed that Gina was no different, but he was surprised by the strength of his disappointment.

He stepped back from her and gave her a cool smile. 'I was wondering if you would like to have dinner with me at my house on Sandbanks?'

The address was a sure-fire winner—reputed to be the fourth most expensive place in the world to live. He had never met a woman yet who had not known that properties on that exclusive part of the Dorset coast were mostly worth in excess of ten million pounds. No doubt Gina would be rather more willing to kiss him now that she realised quite how loaded he was, he thought sardonically.

Lanzo had issued his invitation in a perfectly polite tone, but something in his voice made Gina glad that she had not allowed him to kiss her. The warmth had faded from his eyes, and as she met his hard, glinting green gaze a little shiver ran though her. He was a stranger, her brain reiterated, and there was no reason why she should trust him.

She forced her own polite smile. 'That's very kind of you, but I'm afraid I'm busy every day next week—and as you told me you are only in Poole for a short visit I doubt we will be able to fit dinner into our respective schedules.'

Lanzo stared at Gina in astonishment, hardly able to believe that she had turned him down. It had never happened to him before, and for a moment he was lost for words. He was used to the fact that his looks and wealth were a potent combination which guaranteed him female attention wherever he went. He only had to click his fingers to have any woman who caught his eye. Ten years ago he had recognised that Gina had had a crush on him. She had fallen into his bed with little effort on his part, and if he was honest he had confidently assumed that she would do so again.

But it was not only her appearance that had changed, he mused. At eighteen she had been shy at first with him, but when he had got to know her and she had relaxed with him he had been charmed by her love of life and her cheerful, carefree nature. At that black period of his life she had seemed like a breath of fresh air, and a welcome distraction from the grim memories of his past.

What had happened in the ten years since he had last seen Gina that had robbed her of her youthful exuberance? he wondered. The woman standing before him had appeared sophisticated and self-assured at the party, but now that they were alone she was tense and on edge, watching him warily—as if she expected him to do what…? he wondered with a frown. *Dio,* she was afraid of him, he suddenly realised. She had not pulled away from him because she was playing the coquette, but because she did not trust him.

Outrage caused him to stiffen. What in heaven's name had he done to make her think he might harm her in some way? Following swiftly on the heels of that thought came the realisation that something, or *someone*, from her past must have caused her to change from a fun-loving girl to a woman who was desperately trying to disguise the fact that she was nervous of him. He wanted to ask her *who*? *What* had happened to her that made her flinch from him?

He looked at her tense face and acknowledged that she was not likely to confide in him. More surprising was the feeling of protectiveness that swept through him—together with anger that someone had turned her from the trusting, happy girl he had once known to a woman who was wary and mistrustful, with an air of sadness about her that tugged on his insides.

'What a busy life you must lead if you do not have one free night,' he murmured. 'Perhaps we can postpone my invitation to dinner until my next visit to Poole?' he added softly when she blushed. He held out his hand. 'Give me your key.'

'Why?' Gina could not hide the suspicion in her voice. What did he want? Was he hoping she would invite him in for coffee, and then expect the invitation to lead to something more? Panic churned inside her. Since her divorce she had been on a couple of dinner dates, but she had never been alone with a man. Simon had caused untold damage to her self-confidence, she acknowledged heavily. She wanted to move on, have other relationships and maybe even fall in love, but sometimes she despaired that she would ever be able to trust a man again.

'I was merely going to see you safely inside,' Lanzo explained steadily, taking the key that Gina was clutching in her fingers.

He stood staring down at her for a few moments, and her breath caught in her throat when something flared in his eyes. She wondered if he was going to ignore her earlier plea and kiss her after all, and she realised that part of her wished he would pull her into his arms and slant his sensual mouth over hers. She wanted to forget Simon's cruelty and lose herself in Lanzo's potent magnetism. Unconsciously she moistened her lower lip with the tip of her tongue, and heard his swiftly indrawn breath.

'*Buona notte*, Gina,' he said quietly, and then, to her shock, he turned and walked away, striding along the quay without a single glance over his shoulder. His tall, broad-shouldered figure was gradually swallowed up by the darkness, and the ring of his footsteps faded into the night, leaving her feeling strangely bereft.

For a few moments she stared after him, and then stepped into her flat and shut the door, realising as she did so that she had been holding her breath. Why on earth, she asked herself angrily, did she feel an overwhelming urge to burst into tears? Was it the thought that she would probably never see Lanzo again after she had refused his invitation to dinner? He was a billionaire playboy who could have any woman he wanted and he was not likely to bother with her again.

She was too wound up to go to bed, and after flicking through the TV channels and finding nothing that captured her attention she headed for the bathroom and ran a bath. Lanzo's darkly handsome face filled her consciousness, and with a sigh she sank into the fragrant bubbles and allowed her mind to drift back ten years.

She had been so excited to be offered a job as a waitress at the swanky new Italian restaurant on the quay, Gina recalled. She'd just finished her A-levels and been desperate to earn some money to spend on new summer clothes. While she had been at school she had received a small allowance from her father, but the family farm barely made a profit and money had always been tight.

Lanzo had arrived in Poole for the opening night of the

Di Cosimo restaurant and stayed for the summer. Golden-skinned, exotic, and heart-stoppingly sexy, he had been so far removed from the few boys of her own age Gina had dated that she had been blown away by his stunning looks and lazy charm.

He had a reputation as a playboy, and he'd always had a gorgeous woman clinging to his arm. How she had envied those women, Gina remembered ruefully. How she had longed to be beautiful and blonde and thin. But Lanzo had never seemed to notice her—until one day he had spoken to her and she had been so tongue-tied that she had stared at the floor, praying he would not notice her scarlet face.

'Don't slouch,' he had instructed her. 'You should hold your head up and be confident—not scurry around like a little mouse. When you look down no one can see your eyes, which is a pity because you have beautiful eyes,' he had added slowly, and he had tilted her chin and stared down at her.

She had hardly been able to breathe, and when he had smiled she had practically melted at his feet and smiled shyly back at him. And that had been the start, she thought. From that day Lanzo had made a point of saying hello to her, or bidding her goodnight at the end of her shift. When he had learned that she had to race out of the restaurant when it closed so that she could catch the last bus home he had insisted on driving her back to the farm, and those journeys in his sports car had become the highlight of her days.

Lanzo drove at a hair-raising speed, and that first night Gina had gripped her seat as they had hurtled down the narrow country lanes, the hedgerows flashing past in a blur.

'Relax—I'm a good driver,' he had said in an amused voice. 'Tell me about yourself.'

That had certainly made her forget her fear that he would misjudge the next sharp bend and they would crash. What on earth was there to tell? She'd been sure the mundane details of her life would be of no interest to a playboy billionaire, but she had obediently chatted to him about growing up on the farm with her father and stepmother, and her two stepsisters.

'My parents divorced when I was eight, and when Dad married Linda a few years later she brought her daughters, Hazel and Sarah, to live at the farm.'

'What about your mother?' Lanzo asked. 'Why didn't you live with her after the divorce?'

'Dad thought it would be better for me to stay with him. My mother had been having an affair behind my father's back, and one day I came home from school to find a note saying she had left us for one of the labourers Dad had employed on the farm. Mum never stayed in one place for long, or with one man,' Gina admitted. 'I visited her occasionally, but I was happier living with Dad and Linda.'

Witnessing her mother's chaotic lifestyle and her numerous volatile relationships had made Gina realise that she wanted her future to be very different. Marriage, a happy home and children might not be fashionable goals, but she wasn't ashamed to admit that they were more important to her than a high-flying career.

Lanzo drove her home several times a week, and she slowly grew more relaxed with him—although her intense awareness of him never lessened. He was always charming, but sometimes she sensed a dark mood beneath his smile. There was a restless tension about him, and an air of deep sadness that puzzled and disturbed her, but he never spoke of his personal life and she was too shy to pry.

'I find you peaceful company, Gina,' he told her one night when he stopped the car outside the farm gates.

'Is that a polite way of saying I'm boring?' she blurted out, wishing with all her heart that he thought she was gorgeous and sexy. *Peaceful* made her sound like a nun.

'Of course not. I don't find you at all boring,' he assured her quietly. He turned his head towards her, and the brilliant gleam in his green eyes made Gina's heart lurch. 'You are very lovely,' he murmured deeply, before he brushed his mouth over hers in a kiss that was as soft as thistledown and left her yearning for more.

'I checked the rota and saw that it's your day off tomorrow. Would you like to come out with me on my boat?'

Would she?

She barely slept that night, and the next day when she heard Lanzo's car pull up on the drive she dashed out to meet him, her face pink with an excitement that at eighteen she was too young and naïve to try and disguise.

It had been a glorious day, Gina remembered, sliding deeper beneath the bathwater. The sun had shone from a cloudless blue sky as Lanzo had steered the luxurious motor cruiser he had chartered out of the harbour. His dark mood seemed to have disappeared, and he'd been charismatic and mouth-wateringly sexy, his faded jeans sitting low on his hips and his chest bared to reveal an impressive six-pack. Gina had watched him with a hungry yearning in her eyes, and her heart had raced when he had pulled her into his arms and kissed her.

They had cruised along the coast, picnicked in a secluded bay, and later he had made love to her in the cabin below deck. The sound of the waves lapping against the boat and the mewing cry of the gulls had mingled with his low murmurs of pleasure when he had stroked his hands over her trembling, eager body.

There had been one moment when her hesitancy had

made him pause. 'It's not your first time, is it?' he had asked with a frown.

'No,' she'd lied, terrified that he would stop if she admitted the truth.

But he hadn't stopped. He had kissed her with a feverish passion that had thrilled her, and caressed her with gentle, probing fingers until she had been so aroused that when he had finally entered her there had been no discomfort, just a wonderful sense of completeness—as if she had been waiting all her life for this moment and this man.

The bathwater had cooled, and Gina shivered as she sat up abruptly and reached for a towel. She had not only give Lanzo her virginity that day, she had given him her heart—naïvely not realising that for him sex was simply a pleasurable experience that meant nothing to him. Now she was older and wiser, and she understood that desire and love were not inextricably entwined.

She would not be so careless with her heart again, she thought as she stared at her smudged reflection in the steamed-up mirror. In fact, since her marriage to Simon had proved to be such a mistake, she had lost all confidence in her judgement and wondered if she would ever fall in love again.

But she was not an over-awed eighteen-year-old with a head full of unrealistic expectations, she reminded herself. She knew Lanzo had desired her tonight, and she could not deny her fierce attraction to him. She could not allow her experiences with Simon to ruin the rest of her life, and perhaps a passionate fling with a drop-dead sexy playboy was just what she needed to restore her self-confidence after her divorce? she mused.

But much later that night, when sleep still eluded her, she acknowledged that only a fool played with fire and did not expect to get burned.

CHAPTER THREE

THE *Queen of the East* was a sixty-metre-long luxury yacht owned by a wealthy Arab sheikh, and was currently moored in St Peter Port off the island of Guernsey. The yacht was certainly impressive, Lanzo thought as he steered his powerboat alongside, shrugged out of his waterproof jacket and prepared to climb aboard.

'I'm glad you could make it, my friend,' Sheikh Rashid bin Zayad Hussain greeted him. 'Your business call was successful, I hope?'

'Yes, thank you. But I apologise once again for my lateness,' Lanzo murmured, accepting a glass of champagne from a waiter and glancing around at the other guests who were milling about the yacht's breathtakingly opulent salon. 'The refit is superb, Rashid.'

'I admit I am impressed with the quality of workmanship and attention to detail by Nautica World. The company is small, but Richard Melton has certainly delivered. That is him over there.' The Sheikh dipped his head slightly. 'A pleasant fellow—married with two small children, I believe. He has built his company up from nothing, which is no mean feat in these economic times.'

Lanzo followed the Sheikh's gaze and stiffened with shock. He had been unable to dismiss Gina from his mind for the past twenty-four hours, which had made a mockery of his decision not to contact her again. He desired her, but it was more than that. He was intrigued by her, and curious to discover why she was so different from the girl he had once known.

'Is the woman with Melton his wife?' he demanded tersely.

'The beautiful brunette in the white dress?' Sheikh Hussain looked over at the Englishman, whose hand was resting lightly on his female companion's slender waist. 'No. He simply introduced her as a friend when they came on board. I have met Mrs Melton once, and I understand that she is expecting another child.' To the Sheikh's mind there was only one explanation as to the identity of the mystery woman. 'It would seem that Richard Melton's good taste extends to his choice of mistress,' he murmured.

Lanzo's jaw hardened as he stared at Gina and her male companion. Last night he had puzzled over why she had seemed so wary of him, and had felt concerned that she had been hurt by an event or a person in her past. But now, as he noted her designer dress and the exquisite pearl necklace around her throat, he was sure he had imagined the air of mystery about her, and cynically wondered if she rejected him in favour of a married lover.

'So, what do you think of the yacht?'

Gina glanced at her brother-in-law and grimaced. 'It's stunning, but a bit over the top for my liking,' she replied honestly. 'There's a lot of gold. Do you know that even the taps in the bathroom are gold-plated? Well, of course you know—your company was responsible for the refit. I suppose the important thing is that Sheikh Hussain likes it.'

Richard grinned. 'He loves it—which is why he's throwing a party to show it off. Even better, several of his friends here tonight also own yachts and are interested in having them refitted, which is good news for Nautica World.' He paused. 'Thanks for accompanying me tonight, Gina. The party is a fantastic opportunity to drum up new business. Usually Sarah comes with me, but she's finding the last few weeks of this pregnancy exhausting, and I know she was grateful you agreed to take her place.'

'I'm happy to help,' Gina said easily. Her smile faded as she thought of her stepsister. 'Sarah does seem a bit fed up—but I suppose three pregnancies in four years is a lot to cope with.'

'To be perfectly honest, this last baby was a bit of a mistake,' Richard admitted ruefully. 'I only have to look at Sarah and she falls pregnant,' he joked.

Lucky Sarah, Gina thought wistfully. Her stepsister had no idea what it was like to be unable to conceive, to have your hopes dashed every month, and to feel a pang of longing every time you saw a newborn baby.

She knew her family would have been surprised to learn that she and Simon had tried for over a year to have a child. 'Oh, Gina is a career woman,' they'd explained, whenever the question of babies was mentioned by other relatives. She had never spoken about her infertility; she felt enough of a failure as it was, without her family's well meaning sympathy. And so now she smiled at her brother-in-law and bit back the comment that she would give anything to be happily married with two adorable children and a third on the way.

Richard glanced across the salon. 'You see that man over there?' he murmured. 'He's one of Sheikh Hussain's cousins, and he owns a forty-foot motor cruiser. I think I'll go and have a chat with him.'

Gina laughed. 'I hope you can convince him that he needs Nautica World's services.' She was very fond of her brother-in-law. Richard worked hard, and certainly deserved to be successful.

'You look stunning tonight, *cara*.'

The familiar, sexy drawl caused Gina to spin round, and her heart missed a beat when her eyes clashed with Lanzo's glinting green gaze. Once again his appearance had taken her by surprise, and she had no time to disguise her reaction to him, colour flaring in her cheeks as she acknowledged how incredibly handsome he looked in a black dinner jacket and a snowy white shirt that contrasted with his darkly tanned skin.

'If I'm not mistaken, your dress is a couture creation. Business must be booming if your boyfriend can afford to buy you pearls and designer clothes, as well as supporting his children and a pregnant wife,' he drawled.

Gina stared at him, puzzled by his words and the flare of contempt in his eyes. 'I don't have a boyfriend—married or otherwise,' she told him shortly.

'You're saying that you are not Richard Melton's mistress?'

Shock rendered her speechless for twenty seconds. '*No!* I mean, *yes*. That's exactly what I'm saying.' Twin spots of angry colour flared on Gina's cheeks. 'Of course I'm not Richard's *mistress*.' Her fingers strayed unwittingly to the rope of perfect white pearls around her neck. 'Why on earth would you think that?'

Lanzo's eyes narrowed. 'Sheikh Hussain has met Melton's wife. Why else would he parade you on his arm if you are not lovers?'

'He's my brother-in-law,' she explained angrily. 'Richard is married to my stepsister. Sarah is expecting a baby in a few weeks, and she was too tired to attend the party tonight, so I came with Richard instead.'

She thought of all the newspaper stories she had read

over the years about Lanzo's numerous affairs with glamorous mistresses. The Sheikh was no better. Richard had told her he had a wife in Dubai, but he was obviously having an affair with the voluptuous redhead who was hanging on his arm tonight.

She gave a harsh laugh. 'You and your Sheikh friend might be notorious womanisers, but don't judge everyone by your low standards. Richard is devoted to Sarah and the boys, and I would *never*—' She broke off, suddenly aware that her raised voice was drawing attention from other guests. 'I would never have a relationship with a married man. My necklace was left to me by my grandmother, if you must know,' she said coldly, dismayed to feel her heart-rate quicken when Lanzo ran his fingertip lightly over the pearls and then, by accident or design, traced the line of her collarbone.

'The pearls were a wedding present to Nonna Ginevra from my grandfather, and I'll always treasure them.' Her grandparents had been happily married for sixty years before they had died within a few months of each other. Gina regarded the necklace as a symbol of hope that marriages could last, even though hers had ended after two years. She glared at Lanzo. 'Excuse me, I need some fresh air,' she snapped, and spun round to walk away from him.

She had only taken two steps when a voice called her name.

'Gina—just the person I wanted to see. You'll be pleased to know that I've found tenants who want to rent your flat.'

Gina smiled faintly at Geoffrey Robins, who owned an estate agency in Poole. 'That *is* good news,' she agreed.

'They want to move in at the end of the month, if that suits you. And the rent they are prepared to pay will cover your mortgage repayments. Did you say you were going to move back to your father's place until you find another job?' Geoffrey asked her. 'Only I heard on the grapevine that Peter is putting the farm on the market following his heart attack.'

She nodded. 'Yes, Dad *is* selling the farm. But Sarah and Hazel have both said that I can stay with them, and hopefully I'll find a job soon.' Both her stepsisters had growing families and small houses. Moving in with one or other of them was not going to be ideal, but Gina knew that her only hope of keeping her flat was to rent it out for a few months.

'Well, I'll catch up with you next week and let you know a few more details,' Geoffrey said. His eyes lit up when he saw a waiter approach them. 'Ah, I think I'll have another glass of that excellent Burgundy.' He reached out his hand to take a glass of wine, but as he did so the waiter stumbled, the glasses on the tray shot forward, and Gina gave a cry as red wine cascaded down the front of her dress.

'Scusi! Mi dispiace tanto, signora!' The horrified waiter apologised profusely in his native Italian. The yacht's crew were of a variety of nationalities, and this waiter was young and very good-looking—another heartbreaker in the making, Gina thought wryly.

'E'bene. Non si preoccupy.' It's fine. Don't worry, she assured him calmly.

'Apparently the best way to remove a red wine stain is to cover it in white wine,' Geoffrey advised, handing her a small white handkerchief which was of no use at all.

'I'm quite wet enough, thanks,' Gina said dryly, supremely conscious of the interested glances she was receiving from the other guests.

She *was* annoyed that her dress was probably ruined. Her days of being able to afford expensive clothes, which had been a requirement of her job at Meyers, were over, and she would not be able to replace the dress. But far worse was the knowledge that she was the centre of attention. She frantically scanned the salon for Richard, her heart sinking when she saw that he was still deep in conversation with a potential client.

'Come with me,' a deep, gravelly voice commanded, and before she could think of arguing Lanzo had slipped his hand beneath her elbow and steered her swiftly through the throng of guests out onto the deck.

'I don't believe it,' she muttered as she dabbed ineffectively at the spreading wine stain with the handkerchief. 'Dinner is going to be served in a few minutes. I wonder if the Sheikh has anything I could change into?'

'I doubt it. Rashid probably keeps a selection of skimpy negligees for his mistresses, but you might not feel comfortable wearing one to dinner.'

'You're right. I wouldn't,' Gina muttered, infuriated by the amused gleam in Lanzo's eyes.

'There's only one thing to do. I'll take you home.'

She glanced pointedly at the sea stretching far into the distance. The English coastline was not even visible. 'What a brilliant suggestion,' she said sarcastically. 'The only snag is that I can't swim that far.'

'You don't have to, *cara*. My boat is moored alongside the yacht.'

Frowning, Gina followed Lanzo to the stern of the yacht and stared down at his powerboat. 'I'm not sure...' she said doubtfully.

'Come on.' He was already climbing down the ladder which hung over the side of the yacht, and glanced up at her impatiently. 'Climb down. Don't worry. I'll catch you if you fall.'

Gina hesitated, deeply reluctant to go with Lanzo. Her

heart had leapt the instant she had seen him tonight, and she was irritated that she seemed incapable of controlling her reaction to him. But the red wine had soaked through her dress, and she felt sticky and urgently in need of a shower.

'All right,' she said slowly. 'But you won't go too fast, will you?'

'Of course not,' he assured her smoothly.

It was no easy feat to climb down the ladder in heels and a long skirt, and she gasped when strong hands settled around her waist and Lanzo lowered her into his boat.

'There's not a lot of room.' He stated the obvious as he helped her slide into one of the two front seats, before easing himself behind the wheel. 'Powerboats are designed for speed rather than comfort. Here—slip this around your shoulders,' he told her as he shrugged out of his dinner jacket and handed it to her. 'It might help shield you from the spray.'

His voice was drowned out by the throaty throb of the engine, and as the boat shot forward Gina gripped the edge of her seat and closed her eyes. 'Remember you promised not to go too fast,' she yelled, but her words were whipped away on the wind.

'Didn't you find that exhilarating?' Lanzo demanded, a hair-raising half-hour later, as he cut the throttle and steered the boat alongside a private jetty in Poole Harbour.

Gina unclenched her fingers from the edge of her seat and put a shaky hand up to push the hair out of her eyes. They had sped across the sea so fast that the wind had whipped the clip from her chignon, and now her hair fell in a tangled mass down her back. 'That's not quite how I would describe it,' she said curtly. 'I was terrified.'

'You had no reason to be.' He frowned when he saw how

pale she was. 'I know what I'm doing. You were perfectly safe with me.'

She did not doubt his ability to handle the powerboat, but she did not feel safe with Lanzo even on dry land, Gina admitted to herself. She did not fear that he would hurt her, as Simon had done. Her wariness stemmed from the feelings he evoked in her—the hot, flustered feeling of sexual desire that she had not felt for a very long time.

She looked up at the row of huge houses set back from the jetty and stiffened. 'Why have we come to Sandbanks?' she asked sharply. 'I thought you were going to take me home.'

'I have brought you to my home. My housekeeper will know how to clean that wine stain.' Lanzo had jumped onto the jetty and, ignoring her mutinous expression, swung her into his arms and set her down beside him. 'I want to talk to you.'

'About what?' she demanded suspiciously.

'I have a proposition that I am confident will suit both of us. Come up to the house and we can discuss it,' he ordered, and strode along the jetty, leaving Gina with no option but to trail after him.

Twenty minutes later she emerged from the marble-tiled bathroom Lanzo had shown her to after he had ushered her into his house, feeling considerably cleaner after a shower. She had blasted her hair with a hairdryer and donned a white towelling robe, and now she stepped hesitantly into the main hall, wondering what to do.

'Feeling better?' Lanzo strolled through one of the doors leading off the hall. 'Daphne has prepared us something to eat. Come on through.'

He had discarded his bow tie and unfastened the top few buttons of his shirt to reveal several inches of bronzed skin overlaid with whorls of dark chest hair. Gina's stomach lurched and she took a steadying breath. 'Who is Daphne?'

'My housekeeper, cook and general all-round saint. Daphne travels with me to my various houses around the world, and is the only woman I can't live without,' he told her, his smile revealing his perfect white teeth.

It transpired that Daphne was a tiny, dark-haired woman with a lined brown face and brilliant black eyes. Why on earth did she feel so pleased that Lanzo's housekeeper was not a gorgeous, leggy blonde? Gina asked herself irritably as she followed him into a huge open-plan lounge, with floor-to-ceiling windows that looked out over the sea.

'What an incredible view,' she murmured, distracted from her acute awareness of him for a few moments. 'My flat overlooks the harbour, but the view is nothing as spectacular as this.'

Sliding glass doors opened onto a decked area where a table was laid with a selection of colourful salad dishes and crusty rolls. Of course—they had missed dinner aboard the yacht, Gina remembered, discovering suddenly that she was hungry.

'I didn't know that you speak Italian,' Lanzo commented when they had sat down and he'd indicated that she should help herself to food.

'My grandmother taught me. She moved to England when she married my grandfather, but she missed Italy and loved to speak her own language.'

'Whereabouts in Italy did she come from?'

'Rome.' Gina heaped crispy lettuce leaves onto her plate, and topped them with a slice of round, creamy white mozzarella cheese. 'I've been there several times for work, but never had time to explore the city. One day I plan to go back and look for the house where Nonna used to live.'

'Di Cosimo Holdings' head offices are in Rome.' Lanzo

filled two glasses with wine and handed her one. 'To old friendships and new beginnings,' he murmured, touching his glass to hers.

'Oh…yes…' Gina hesitated fractionally. 'To old friendships.' She wasn't convinced about new beginnings, and to avoid his speculative gaze she took a sip of deliciously cool Chardonnay.

'Come and work for me and I promise I'll give you a guided tour of the city. I know Rome well, and I'm sure I'll be able to find your grandmother's house.'

Her eyes flew to his face. She had been so absorbed in her intense awareness of him last night that she had forgotten his offer for her to work for him as a temporary PA. Now she hurriedly shook her head. 'No—I don't think so.'

'Why are you so quick to dismiss the idea?' Lanzo sat back and studied her broodingly. 'And why do you need to rent out your flat?'

'Were you eavesdropping on my conversation with Geoffrey?' Gina began hotly.

'I was standing close by and couldn't help but overhear.'

She was tempted to tell him to mind his own business, but after a moment she shrugged and put down her fork, her appetite fading as it always did when she remembered her financial worries.

'When I moved back to Poole I took out a big mortgage to buy my flat,' she admitted. 'It wasn't a problem at the time, because I was earning a good salary at Hartman Homes, but since I lost my job I've fallen behind with the repayments.'

'I'm prepared to offer you a six-month contract and pay you a generous salary—higher than you were earning at Meyers.'

Gina's brows lifted. 'That's a rather rash statement when you don't *know* what I earned at Meyers.'

'I have a fair idea. A good PA is like gold-dust, and I expect to pay good money to ensure the best staff.'

'How do you know I'm good at my job?'

He shrugged. 'I checked your references. Did you think I would offer you the vital role of my personal assistant without first making sure you could handle the responsibility?' he queried coolly when she opened her mouth to tell him he had a nerve. 'I am a businessman, *cara*, and I never allow emotions to dictate my decisions.

'I spoke to your previous boss, Frank Wallis, and he assured me that you were the most dedicated and efficient PA he'd ever had—with an almost obsessive attention to detail,' Lanzo added, looking amused. 'Apparently you had a complicated system of colour-coded notes.'

Gina flushed. 'I like to be organised,' she defended herself. Maybe she *was* a bit obsessive, but she wasn't a control freak as Simon had accused her of being. She simply liked things to run like clockwork.

'I have no problem with you being organised,' Lanzo assured her. 'In fact it is a necessity. I work long hours and travel extensively. I will expect you to accompany me on business trips and also to act as my hostess occasionally when I hold social functions.'

He was going way too fast, Gina thought frantically, panic flaring inside her that he seemed to think her agreement was a given. '*If* I accept the job,' she muttered.

'Why wouldn't you?' he demanded.

There were so many reasons, but the main one was her strong attraction to Lanzo—an attraction that she had decided during a sleepless night that she dared not take any further. He had broken her heart once, and she was not prepared to risk her peace of mind by becoming involved with him again.

But it would only be for six months, a voice in her head pointed out. His job offer was a fantastic opportunity for her to sort out her finances and ensure that she kept her flat that she loved. If she went to Italy to work for Lanzo she would not have to impose herself on her stepsisters while she rented the flat out, and the six months' rent paid by the tenants would cover the mortgage repayments. On top of that she would have six months of earning a high salary that she could put away to cover the mortgage when she returned to Poole and looked for another job.

But move to Rome, work closely with Lanzo every day, and travel to business meetings around the world with him? She chewed on her bottom lip, torn between the temptation of solving her financial problems that were growing worse with every day that she failed to find a job in Poole and fear of what she could be letting herself in for if she agreed.

What would she do if he tried to kiss her again, as he had almost done last night? She swallowed as she met his gaze and saw the banked-down flames of desire smouldering in his striking green eyes. A little tremor ran through her at the knowledge that he was attracted to her. Would it be such a disaster if she responded to him? her mind queried.

Her breath hitched in her throat as his eyes strayed down to the slopes of her breasts, visible where the edges of her robe had parted slightly. Time seemed to be suspended, and she was acutely conscious that her white dress, which was now being cleaned by Lanzo's housekeeper, had not required her to wear a bra. Her breasts felt swollen and heavy, and into her mind came the stark image of Lanzo pushing the robe over her shoulders and lowering his head to take one nipple and then its twin in his mouth.

'You would be a fool to turn me down, Gina.' His voice

jerked her back to reality and she tore her gaze from him, hot colour storming into her cheeks as she prayed he had not guessed her shocking thoughts. 'You need this job, and I need to appoint a temporary PA as soon as possible. I have excellent contacts, and when Luisa returns to work after her maternity leave I will recommend you to other company directors who may be looking for staff.'

It was an offer no sensible person could refuse. A golden chance to keep her flat, which was more than just a home but also a place where she felt safe and secure after two years of living on the edge of her nerves with Simon. She had hoped that buying the flat would be the start of a new chapter in her life—a mark of her independence now that she had escaped her violent marriage. She had vowed to take any job she could find to meet the mortgage repayments, she reminded herself. She was twenty-eight, no longer a naïve girl, and she was more than capable of dealing with her inconvenient attraction to Lanzo.

'All right,' she said quickly, before she could change her mind. 'I accept your offer.'

Lanzo was careful to hide the feeling of satisfaction that surged through him. He had realised when he had seen Gina on the yacht earlier tonight that his desire for her was too strong for him to be able to dismiss it. He wanted her, and his instincts told him that she was not as immune to him as she would like him to think. But he sensed her wariness, although he did not understand the reason for it, and knew that he would have to be patient and win her trust before he could persuade her into his bed.

'Good,' he said briskly. 'I'll pick you up from your flat at nine tomorrow morning, and my private jet will collect us from Bournemouth airport and take us to Rome. Luisa will come into the office for a couple of hours to run through everything with you.'

Gina gave him a startled look, doubts already forming thick and fast in her head. 'I'll need a few days to get myself organised. For a start I'll have to find somewhere to stay in Rome.'

'You can stay at my apartment. It will be ideal,' he insisted when she opened her mouth to object. 'I often work late in the evenings, and it will be useful to have you on hand. I hope you weren't thinking that this was going to be a nine-to-five job?' Lanzo said abruptly, noticing her doubtful expression. 'For the money I'll be paying you I will expect your full and exclusive attention twenty-four-seven.'

'Presumably my nights will be my own?' she replied coolly, stung by his tone. She was well aware that the job of PA to the head of a global company meant working extended hours, including evenings and weekends when required, but she would need to sleep!

Lanzo leaned back in his chair and surveyed her with a wicked gleam in his eyes. 'Certainly—if you want them to be, *cara*,' he murmured softly. Was she aware of the hungry glances she had been darting at him across the table? he wondered. Or the way the pulse at the base of her throat was jerking frantically beneath her skin?

Under ordinary circumstances he would not consider mixing his work with his personal life. Office relationships always created problems, which was why he never had affairs with his staff. But the current circumstances were not ordinary.

It had come as a bolt from the blue when his PA of the last five years had suddenly announced that she was getting married, and then a few months later revealed that she was pregnant. Of course he was pleased for Luisa—although somewhat surprised, because she had never given any indication that she wanted to settle down to a life of domestic bliss. But he resented the disruption her pregnancy had caused to his life. Two junior secretaries had jointly taken over organising his diary, but he missed Luisa's calm efficiency that had ensured his office ran as smoothly as a well-oiled machine.

His conversation with Gina's retired boss from Meyers had convinced him that she was ideally suited to fill the position of his temporary PA. But, more than that, it was a chance for him to get to know her again. She had lingered in his mind for a long time after he had returned to Italy ten years ago. They had been friends as well as lovers, and now it was perfectly natural for him be intrigued by her, he assured himself.

It went without saying that any relationship he might have with her would not involve his emotions. After the fire fifteen years ago had taken everyone he had loved he had felt frozen inside. His heart was as cold and hard as a lump of ice, and he was not sure than anything would ever make it thaw.

CHAPTER FOUR

'WHAT was the name of that little country pub in the New Forest that we used to go to?' Lanzo queried. 'Do you remember it? We went there several times.'

Of course she remembered, Gina thought silently. She remembered every place she had visited with Lanzo ten years ago. 'It was the Hare and Hounds, famous for its steak and ale pies,' she told him. 'You took me there for lunch on my days off from the restaurant.'

'Mmm—and afterwards we went walking in the forest.'

They had walked deep among the trees and made love in a little clearing, where the sun had filtered through the leafy canopy above and dappled their bodies. Gina inhaled sharply. 'Yes, we went on some lovely walks,' she murmured, pretending to clear her throat to disguise the huskiness of her voice. 'The New Forest is very pretty.'

'We made love in a little dell, hidden among the trees.' Lanzo stretched his long legs out in front of him and turned his head towards Gina, his mouth curving into a sensual smile when she blushed. 'Do you remember, *cara*?'

'Vaguely.' She affected an uninterested shrug. 'It was a long time ago.' She stared out of the window of Lanzo's private jet at the endless expanse of brilliant blue sky, and tried to ignore her fierce awareness of him. It wasn't easy when he was sitting next to her, his body half turned to hers so that her eyes were drawn to his face, and inevitably, to the sensual curve of his mouth.

She had only spent three hours in his company since he had picked her up from her flat that morning, but she was already losing the battle to remain immune to his charisma, she thought dismally. When he had taken the seat next to her on the plane she had assumed he would open his laptop and catch up on some work, but instead he had spent the entire flight chatting to her and reminiscing about the past.

To be honest she was surprised at how much he remembered of their affair. They had only been lovers for a matter of weeks, yet Lanzo recalled the places they had visited together, as well as those passionate sex sessions in the forest, which were branded indelibly in her memory but which she'd thought he had forgotten.

'How much longer until we land?' she asked him briskly. Perhaps once they were at the Di Cosimo offices in Rome she would be able to slip into the role of efficient PA, and her heart would stop leaping every time he smiled at her?

'We won't be long now. The pilot has just indicated that we should fasten our seatbelts,' he told her, his eyes glinting with amusement when she gave an audible sigh of relief.

Rome in late June was stiflingly hot; the temperature displayed on the information board at Fiumcino Airport showed thirty-two degrees Celsius, and Gina was glad to slide into the cool interior of Lanzo's waiting limousine.

'We'll go straight to the office,' he told her as the car moved smoothly into the stream of traffic heading in the direction of the city centre. 'Luisa is going to be there to hand over to you. This afternoon I'm holding a board meeting and I'll require you to take the minutes.'

As he spoke his phone bleeped, and he began to scroll

through his messages while simultaneously checking emails on his laptop. The powerboat racer playboy had been replaced by the powerful billionaire businessman, Gina mused. Dressed in a beautifully tailored dark grey suit, blue silk shirt, and toning tie, he was achingly sexy. She sighed and tore her eyes from him. She had barely slept last night, plagued by doubts over her decision to work for him. She had no qualms about her ability to cope with the demands of the job of his PA, but she was less confident about her ability to deal with the devastating affect he had on her peace of mind.

'I'm afraid my Italian might be a bit rusty,' she said worriedly. 'I spent six months working for an Italian company in Milan, but that was before...' She had been about to say *before I got married*, but she had no desire to talk about Simon—her marriage had been a bleak period of her life she preferred to forget. 'That was a few years ago,' she said instead. 'You'll have to ask your board members to be patient with me.'

'Don't worry about it. Di Cosimo Holdings is a global company and the board members are not all Italian. Meetings are usually conducted in English,' Lanzo explained.

Privately, he did not think the members of the board would be overly concerned with Gina's language skills and were far more likely to focus their attention on her curvaceous figure. Presumably her aim had been to look smart and efficient, in a pale grey suit teamed with a lilac-coloured blouse, but the pencil skirt moulded her derrière so that it swayed delightfully when she walked, and the cut of her jacket emphasised her slender waist and her full breasts. Long, slim legs sheathed in sheer hose, and high-heeled black stilettos completed her outfit, and the whole effect was one of understated elegance that could not hide the fact that Gina was a sexy and desirable woman.

Lanzo took a sharp breath. He had spent the entire flight fantasising about leading Gina into the bedroom at the rear of the plane and unbuttoning that prim blouse. He could see the faint outline of her lacy bra beneath it, and in the fantasy he had peeled the straps over her shoulders so that her ample breasts spilled into his hands. Patience was all very well, but his determination to take things slowly was already wearing thin, and he was wondering how quickly he could persuade her to lower her barriers. One thing was certain: he would have to subtly let it be known to his board members that his temporary PA was off-limits to anyone but him, he decided.

'I'm sure it won't take you long to settle in,' he murmured. 'Do you like pizza?'

'I love it—unfortunately.' Gina grimaced. 'I'm afraid my hips don't need any encouragement to expand.'

'You look in perfect proportion to me.' Lanzo subjected her to a leisurely inspection that made her feel hot and flustered. 'I agree you're not a bag of bones, in the way so many women seem to think is attractive, but you won't find any complaints here in Italy, *cara*. Italian men like their women to be curvaceous. At least…' He paused and trapped her gaze with his mesmeric green eyes. 'At least this Italian male does.'

He was blatantly flirting with her, Gina realised, irritated by her body's instinctive reaction to him. She wanted to tell him to back off—that the hungry gleam in his eyes was totally inappropriate when she was one of his employees.

What chance did she stand of resisting him when he turned on his full mega-watt charm? she thought despairingly. But Lanzo could not help flirting with women—all women. It was as natural to him as breathing, and it didn't mean anything. The best way to deal with it was to ignore it, she told herself firmly.

'Why did you want to know if I like pizza?' she said lightly. 'Were you going to recommend a good restaurant?'

'Agnelli's—it's a little place tucked away down a side-street, off the main tourist trail, and it serves the best pizza in Rome. I thought we could eat there tonight.'

'Please don't feel you have to entertain me,' Gina said quickly. 'I'm sure you have a busy social life, and I'm quite happy to do my own thing.'

His smile made her heart flip. 'But we are old friends, Gina,' he said softly. 'I want to spend time with you.'

Oh, hell! Did he have any idea how emotive she found the expression *old friends*? How it tugged on her heart and sent her mind spinning back to those few weeks many years ago when she had been so insanely happy? Perhaps the happiest she had ever been in her life, a little voice inside her head whispered.

The atmosphere inside the car suddenly seemed taut with tension. The rumble of traffic outside faded, and Gina was painfully conscious of the ragged sound of her breathing. Coming to Italy with him had been a mistake, she thought frantically. Yet she could not deny that she felt more alive than she had felt for a long, long time.

She could not tear her eyes from his mouth, and memories filled her mind of him kissing her with hungry passion all those years ago. His reminiscing over their affair had made her remember how gentle he had been with her the first time he had made love to her. Her ex-husband had rarely been tender, and had taken his own pleasure with selfish disregard for hers. Her unsatisfying sex life had been one of the first disappointments of her marriage, Gina thought ruefully. She had not known in those early days how much worse her relationship with Simon would become.

Every instinct she possessed told her that Lanzo was nothing like Simon and that he would never hurt her—not physically, at any rate. It was the threat he posed to her emotional security that worried her. When his mouth curved into a slow smile everything flew from her mind but her yearning for him to brush his lips over hers and then deepen the kiss until he obliterated all her fears.

She caught her breath when he leaned towards her, but then he stilled and she felt sick inside, knowing that he had noticed her scar. She had been in such a rush that morning, at the last minute frantically packing belongings she had thought she would need in Italy, and she had not taken as much care as usual to conceal her scar with make-up. She tried to jerk away from him, but he slid his hand beneath her chin and gently forced her to look at him.

'That must have been a nasty wound,' he said quietly. 'What happened?'

'I had an accident a year or so ago,' she muttered, pulling her hair around her face to cover the scar. She swallowed. 'It's horrible. It makes me feel so ugly.'

Lanzo gave her a puzzled look. 'What kind of accident—a car crash?' He hazarded a guess. The scar was a long thin line that ran down her face, beneath her ear and a little way down her neck. He could only think that she had been cut—perhaps by glass when a windscreen had shattered.

Gina shook her head. 'It's not important.' The matter of how she had gained her scar was absolutely off-limits. She never spoke of it to anyone—not even her family.

Lanzo hesitated, and then said matter-of-factly, 'It hardly shows, and it certainly does not make you look ugly, *cara*. Nothing could diminish your beauty.'

His smile deepened as she gave him a startled glance.

When she blushed she reminded him of the shy waitress who had had a crush on him years ago, who had responded to him with such sweet passion when he had kissed her. He wondered what she would do if he kissed her now. Probably she would jerk away from him like a frightened doe, as she had done when he had walked her home from the Di Cosimo restaurant in Poole. He would like to meet whoever was responsible for causing the fearful look in her eyes, Lanzo thought grimly.

The car came to a halt and Gina released a shaky breath as the chauffeur opened the door for her to step out onto the pavement. Minutes later she followed Lanzo through the tinted glass doors of Di Cosimo Holdings. She was acutely conscious of him as they silently rode the lift up to the top floor, and her hand strayed unwittingly to the long scar hidden beneath her hair as she remembered how he had told her she was beautiful *after* he had seen the unsightly bluish line.

Perhaps her overwhelming awareness of Lanzo was not so surprising. He had been her first lover, and sex with him had been utterly fulfilling. Was it so wrong to want to experience the pleasure of his lovemaking again? To revel in his hard, muscular body skilfully possessing hers, and to make love to him in return—two people meeting as equals and taking each other to the heights of sexual ecstasy?

The lift halted, and as the door slid open she forced her turbulent thoughts to the back of her mind. Now was not an appropriate time to be imagining Lanzo's naked aroused body. *Was* there an appropriate time? she wondered wildly. She had come to Italy to work for him, and she was determined to fulfil the role of his PA with quiet professionalism, she reminded herself firmly.

'Welcome to Di Cosimo Holdings. Come and meet my team,' Lanzo said smoothly. His eyes lingered speculatively on her flushed face, but, calling on all her acting skills, Gina gave him a cool smile and followed him into his office.

Despite being heavily pregnant, Luisa Bartolli was still incredibly elegant, as so many continental women were, Gina thought to herself. Lanzo's PA was also friendly and welcoming, and clearly relieved to meet her temporary replacement.

'Lanzo wasn't impressed when I told him I would be having a few months off to have a baby,' Luisa confided as she gave Gina a tour of the offices. 'I've been his PA for over five years, and I know how much he dislikes any disruption to his routine. But it can't be helped.' She shrugged. 'Until I met my husband I had no plans to marry or have children. But Marco was keen to have a family, and I'm so excited about the baby. I'm thirty-six, and I know I'm lucky to have conceived the first month we tried. I haven't dared mention it to Lanzo yet, but I'm already thinking that I don't want to come back to work full-time and put the baby in day care.' Luisa added. She glanced at Gina. 'I'm sure that with your experience as a PA you'll get on fine working for him. Perhaps you would consider job-sharing with me after my maternity leave is over?'

'I don't think so,' Gina replied hastily. She already had doubts about the wisdom of agreeing to spend the next six months working for Lanzo. She certainly did not plan to extend her time with him. 'I have a flat back in England, and I need to work full-time to pay my mortgage.' She smiled at Luisa. 'Everything seems straightforward, but thanks for saying that I can ring you if I have any problems.' She stared wistfully at Luisa's bump. 'When is the baby due?'

'Not for another six weeks.' Luisa grimaced. 'I feel fine,

but the doctor has told me to rest, and Marco won't allow me to do *anything*. He only allowed me to come into the office today after I promised to spend the rest of the day with my feet up.'

'Your husband is obviously determined to take good care of you,' Gina murmured, stifling a little stab of envy. Her marriage to Simon had been in trouble barely months after the wedding. The charming man who had wined and dined her for six months before he had whisked her away for a romantic weekend in Paris and proposed at the top of the Eiffel Tower had changed overnight, it had seemed, into a possessive husband of unpredictable moods who had been jealous of her friendships and subjected her to verbal abuse when he was drunk.

It was probably a good thing that she had failed to fall pregnant, Gina conceded. Simon's increasing dependence on alcohol meant that he would not have been a good father. She had tried to help him, but it was impossible to help someone who refused to recognise he had a problem, and in the end, for the sake of her sanity and increasingly her physical safety, she had left him.

After Luisa had left, Gina got straight down to business and quickly became absorbed in the pile of paperwork on her desk. It felt good to be back at work. She was not naturally idle, and had hated her enforced weeks of inactivity after she had lost her job in Poole.

She took the minutes of the board meeting, relieved to find that the board members were indeed a mixture of nationalities and everyone spoke English, so her fluency in Italian was not put to the test on her first day. Lanzo had further meetings booked for the rest of the day, but at five he called her into his office and told her that he had arranged for his driver to take her back to his apartment.

'You've done enough for today,' he said, when she

protested that she was happy to stay on until he had finished. 'Go and relax for a couple of hours and I'll meet you at home later.'

Trying not to dwell on the fact that she would be sharing his home for the next few months, she arrived at his penthouse apartment, close to the famous Spanish Steps, and was greeted by Daphne.

'I have unpacked for you,' the housekeeper explained as she led the way to the guest bedroom which, like all the other rooms in the apartment, was decorated in neutral colours. It was not a very homely home—more like a five-star hotel, Gina mused as she glanced around at the ultra-modern décor. Her thoughts must have shown on her face, because Daphne explained, 'Lanzo's real home is his villa on the Amalfi Coast. He only stays here when he needs to be at the head office. Would you like a cup of English tea? He told me to buy it especially for you, because he remembered that you always used to drink it.'

Don't read too much into it, Gina told herself firmly. She smiled at the housekeeper. 'Tea would be lovely, thank you.'

When Daphne had gone she made a quick inspection of her room and the *en suite* bathroom, and then stripped out of her work clothes and stepped into the shower. Ten minutes later she pulled on a cool white cotton sundress, collected her tea from the kitchen, and wandered out onto the roof terrace—a leafy oasis of potted plants with spectacular views across Rome.

She would find her grandmother's house while she was here, Gina decided. It was exciting to be in the historical city, and she was looking forward to playing tourist and visiting the ancient landmarks. For the first time in months she felt her spirits lift—and if her excitement stemmed mainly from the fact that she would be spending the next few months with Lanzo, then so be it, she thought defensively. She was a grown woman and she could look after herself.

An hour later she stirred at the sound of her name, and opened her eyes to find Lanzo standing beside the lounger where she had fallen asleep.

'You should have sat beneath the parasol,' he told her, hunkering down beside her and running his fingers lightly up her arm. 'At this time of the year the sun is still strong until late in the evening, and your fair skin could easily burn.'

'I didn't mean to go to sleep,' she mumbled, jerking upright and pushing her hair back from her hot face. 'I was going to finish typing up the notes from the board meeting.' She stared at him dazedly, her brain still fogged with sleep, and her heart rate quickened when she saw that he had changed into faded jeans and a tight fitting black tee shirt that moulded his broad chest. His hair was still damp from where he had showered, and his hypnotic green eyes gleamed with a hunger he made no effort to disguise. 'When did you get back?' she mumbled, unable to drag her eyes from the chiselled perfection of his handsome face.

'Ten minutes ago.' Lanzo did not add that he had been impatient for his meeting to finish so that he could come home to her. In her simple summer dress she did not look much older than she had at eighteen, he brooded, fighting the urge to tangle his fingers in her long, silky chestnut hair and tilt her head so that he could claim her mouth in a kiss that he knew would not be enough for either of them.

But the faint wariness in her blue eyes cautioned him to bide his time. Gina could not hide her desire for him, however much she tried, but something was holding her back, and he was prepared to wait until she had dealt with whatever demons were bothering her.

'Now that you're awake, are you ready to sample the finest pizza in Rome?' he asked lightly. He held out his hand and, after hesitating for a moment, she placed her fingers in his and allowed him to pull her to her feet. 'Let's go and eat, *cara*. I don't know about you, but I'm starving.'

As Lanzo had said, Agnelli's pizzeria was off the tourist track, tucked away down a narrow side-street that they had reached after a fifteen-minute walk through Rome. From the outside the peeling paint around the front window and the restaurant's air of general shabbiness was not inviting, but when they walked in they were greeted warmly by the staff. Signor Agnelli hurried out of the kitchen, the apron tied around his girth dusty with white flour, and pulled Lanzo into a bear-hug, before ushering them over to a table set in a quiet corner, which he clearly reserved for his close friends.

'Enrico and I go back a long way,' Lanzo confirmed when Gina commented that the restaurant-owner seemed to regard him as a long-lost brother. He did not add that Enrico Agnelli had been one of the first firemen to arrive at the di Cosimo home in Positano on the night of the fire, and that the fireman had almost lost his life trying to save Cristina and Lanzo's parents. The injuries he had received had meant that he had had to leave the fire service, and Lanzo had willingly given his financial backing to help Enrico move to Rome and open the pizzeria.

'That was truly the best pizza I've ever eaten,' Gina said as she finished her last mouthful and sat back in her chair with a contented sigh.

'I'll tell Enrico—he'll be pleased.'

Lanzo's smile made her heart lurch, and she took a hurried sip of her wine, but nothing could distract her from her acute awareness of him, Gina acknowledged ruefully.

He had ignored the cutlery on the table and eaten his pizza with his hands, his evident enjoyment of the food somehow innately sensual. She had been happy to follow suit, and as she'd licked a smear of tomato sauce from her finger she had glanced across the table and found him watching with an intentness that had sent heat coursing through her veins.

They wandered back to his apartment in relaxed silence, and as Gina stared up at the stars glinting in the velvet blackness of the sky she felt a curious lightness inside that she realised with a jolt of shock was sheer happiness. She hadn't thought about Simon and the miserable months when their divorce had become increasingly acrimonious all day. Instead her mind had been full of Lanzo. Sitting across the table from him in Angelli's, she had found herself imagining him *sans* his shirt and hip-hugging jeans, and had pictured the two of them naked on a bed, his bare golden skin gleaming like satin, his powerful arousal rock-hard as he lowered himself onto her...

As the lift whisked them up to the penthouse she could not bring herself to look at him, conscious that her cheeks were burning. Out of the corner of her eye she saw him lift his hand, and stiffened when he lightly touched her arm. Only then did she realise that the strap of her sundress and slipped over her shoulder, revealing a lot more of the upper slope of her breast than she deemed decent. She held her breath when he tugged the strap back into place, and his drawled, 'I'm sure you don't want to fall out of your dress, *cara*,' made her face burn even hotter.

What if, instead of pulling her dress strap up, he had drawn it lower, until he had bared her breast, then shaped it with his palm, stroked his finger over her nipple...?

Her legs felt weak as she followed him into the apartment. Get a grip, she told herself furiously. But she could not control her body's response to Lanzo. He evoked feelings inside her she had thought were dead, had awoken her sexual desires so that for the first time in almost two years she felt a hot, damp yearning between her legs.

'Would you like a drink?' he asked as he ushered her into the lounge. 'A brandy—or I can make you a cup of tea?' Lanzo's eyes narrowed speculatively on Gina's flushed face. Did she know that he could decipher every one of the thoughts that darkened her blue eyes to the colour of midnight? he brooded, hunger and frustration coiling in his gut when she quickly shook her head.

'I think I'll go straight to bed. It's been a long day.' And she was going to make a complete fool of herself if she remained with him for a second longer. 'Goodnight,' she mumbled, and shot down the hallway to her bedroom, closing the door behind her and finally releasing the breath that had been trapped in her lungs.

Things could not continue like this, Gina decided after she had changed into her nightdress, brushed her teeth and climbed into bed—only to find that sleep was impossible while she was imagining Lanzo in his room just along the hall, stripping out of his clothes and sliding into his bed. Did he still sleep naked, as he had done ten years ago? Stop it, she ordered herself, punching her pillows into a more comfortable shape for the umpteenth time.

An hour later she was still wide awake, and now she was thirsty. Knowing that she would never be able to sleep until she'd had a drink, she slid out of bed and stepped into the hall. Everywhere was in darkness, and she assumed Lanzo had gone to bed, but when she pushed open the kitchen door her heart jerked against her ribs at the sight of him leaning against the worktop, idly skimming through a newspaper. He was naked apart from the towel hitched around his waist, and droplets of water glistened on his shoulders and his damp hair, indicating that he had recently showered.

Dear heaven, he was gorgeous! He lowered the paper as Gina hovered in the doorway, his bright green eyes gleaming with amusement when she stared simply stared at him, her mouth open in a perfect *oh* of shock.

Dark eyebrows winged upwards. 'Did you want something, *cara*?'

She moistened her dry lips with her tongue, and the gleam in his eyes became intent and feral. 'I came to get a drink. I usually take a glass of water to bed with me,' she croaked.

'Lucky water,' he murmured, so softly that she wasn't sure she had heard him right. He took a glass from the cabinet, filled it from the tap, and strolled towards her. Her eyes hovered on his towel and she prayed it was securely fastened.

'Here.' He handed her the glass.

'Thank you.'

Leave now, her brain insisted urgently. But her senses were swamped by his closeness, the tantalising scent of clean, damp skin, the sensual musk of his aftershave, and something else that was irrevocably male and primitive that made every nerve-ending in her body tingle.

Green eyes meshed with sapphire-blue. 'Is there anything else you want, Gina?'

His breath whispered across her lips, and without conscious thought she parted them in silent invitation. Lanzo made a muffled sound deep in his throat as he lowered his head and grazed his mouth gently over hers.

It felt like heaven. Starbursts of colour exploded in her mind as he tasted her with delicate little sips, until he felt the little shiver of pleasure that ran through her and deepened the kiss. His lips were warm and firm, yet incredibly gentle, teasing hers apart, his tongue tracing their shape but not sliding into her mouth. Instinctively she leaned closer to him. He lifted his hand and threaded his fingers through her hair.

And then suddenly, from nowhere, Simon's image hurtled into her mind—a memory of him grabbing her hair and pulling several strands from her scalp during one of his drunken rages.

'No!' She jerked away from Lanzo so forcefully that she banged the back of her head on the doorframe. He frowned and lowered his hand. She could see the questions forming on his lips and she shook her head, silently telling him that she was not about to give an explanation for her behaviour. 'I can't.' Her voice was thick with misery. 'I'm sorry.'

She was still clutching the glass, and she spun away from him so urgently that water sloshed over the rim, soaking through her nightdress as she tore down the hall towards her room.

Lanzo watched her go, half tempted to follow her and demand to know what she was playing at. She had turned from soft and willing to tense and *frightened* in the space of a few seconds, and he wanted to know why. But he recalled the expression in her eyes—a silent plea for him to back off—and after a moment he switched off the kitchen light and padded down the hall to his own room, wondering what had happened in her past that had decimated her trust.

CHAPTER FIVE

GINA dreaded facing Lanzo the following morning, but to her relief he greeted her with a casual smile when she joined him on the terrace for breakfast, and made no reference to what had happened between them the previous night. If he was curious as to why she had reacted so badly when he had kissed her he did not allow it to show, and over coffee and the delicious herb and parmesan *frittatas* that Daphne served them he focused exclusively on work and the meetings planned for the day ahead.

A week later, Gina glanced around the quaint little courtyard tucked away down a side-street in the Campo di Fiori area of Rome, and then studied the faded photograph in her hand.

'I'm sure this is where Nonna Ginevra used to live,' she said excitedly. 'The fountain in the centre of the square is just the same, and that house over in the corner looks like the one my grandparents are standing in front of in the photo. It's amazing—this courtyard has hardly changed in over sixty years,' she murmured.

Lanzo peered over her shoulder at the photograph. 'Your grandfather is in military uniform, so I assume the picture must have been taken during the Second World War?'

Gina nodded. 'Grandad was stationed in Italy in the

war, and that's when he met Nonna. They married soon after the war ended, and she moved to the farm in Dorset with him, but she often spoke of her childhood home in Rome. It must have been hard for her to leave the place she loved, but she always said that she loved my grandfather so much that she would have lived on the moon with him if he'd asked her.'

It was hot in the enclosed courtyard, and she sat down on the stone wall surrounding the fountain, glad of the fine spray that cooled her skin.

Lanzo dropped down next to her. 'You were obviously very fond of your grandmother.'

'Yes, I was close to both my grandparents. After my mother left I spent a lot of time with them while Dad was busy on the farm. They died within a few months of each other, and although I was sad I couldn't help but be glad that they were together again,' she said softly. 'Even death didn't part them for long.'

Her grandparents' long and devoted relationship had epitomised all that marriage truly meant, she thought. Love, friendship, respect—the things she had hoped for when she had married Simon, until his drinking binges and increasingly aggressive behaviour had killed her feelings for him.

'I can't believe we've actually found Nonna's childhood home,' she said, refusing to dwell on dark memories when the sun was blazing from a cobalt blue sky. 'You seem to know every corner and backstreet of the city. Did you grow up in Rome?'

Lanzo shook his head. 'No, I was born in Positano, on the Amalfi Coast. I like Rome, and I spend a lot of time here because Di Cosimo Holdings is based here, but home is very much my villa on the clifftops, looking out over the sea.'

'I've heard that the Amalfi Coast is supposed to be one of the most beautiful places in the world,' Gina said, smiling at his enthusiasm. 'Do your family still live there?'

'I have no family. My parents died many years ago, and I was an only child.' Lanzo's tone was curiously emotionless, and his eyes were shaded by his sunglasses so that Gina could not read his expression, but something warned her that he would not welcome further questions about his family.

'I'm sorry,' she murmured. She remembered reading somewhere that he had assumed control of Di Cosimo Holdings when he had been only twenty—long before he had stayed in Poole ten years ago. Presumably he had taken over the company on the death of his father. No wonder he seemed so *detached*, she mused, trying to think of a suitable word to describe him. From the sound of it he had no one in his life he cared about, and perhaps losing his parents when he had been a young man had hardened him.

There was a proverb that stated 'no man is an island'. But Lanzo seemed to prize his independence above anything, and did not appear to need anyone. His housekeeper Daphne ran his various homes and took care of his domestic arrangements, and a ready supply of willowy blonde models satisfied his high sex-drive. She wondered if he had ever been in love, but when she darted a glance at his stern profile she dared not ask, feeling fairly certain what his answer would be.

'Now that we have found where your grandmother used to live, where would you like to visit next?' he asked after a few minutes. 'We're not far from the Piazza Navona, where the fountains are rather more spectacular than this one.' He dipped his hand in the small fountain and flicked water at her, grinning when she yelped. 'The square is world-famous, and the statues are truly worth seeing.'

'You don't have to be my tour guide all weekend,' Gina told him. 'You've already shown me so much of Rome.'

Her mind re-ran the past wonderful week. After her initial awkwardness with him that first morning she had slipped into the role of his PA with surprising ease, and a companionable relationship had quickly developed between them—although she was always conscious of the shimmering sexual chemistry simmering beneath their polite conversations.

Each evening they returned to his apartment to sample Daphne's divine cooking, and afterwards strolled around the city, admiring the exquisite architecture of the ancient landmarks and discovering secret little side-streets and courtyards where they drank Chianti beneath the striped awnings of some of the cafés.

Rome was a magical place, but in her heart Gina recognised that for her the magic was created by Lanzo as he walked close beside her, or smiled indulgently when she paused to study a pretty window box or peer into a shop window. It would be very easy to fall for him, she thought ruefully. And it was that knowledge which held her back from responding to the sultry invitation in his eyes each time she bade him goodnight every evening and went to her bedroom to sleep alone.

She was puzzled that, although he did not try to disguise the fact that he desired her, he had made no further attempt to kiss her. She supposed she should have felt reassured that he was obviously not going to pressure her in any way, but instead she lay awake every night, gripped by a restless longing as she imagined his muscular, naked body pressing down on her soft flesh, his dark head lowered to her breast.

'I've enjoyed showing you around,' he told her, his voice cutting through her erotic fantasy, so that she blushed scarlet and hastily avoided his gaze. 'We won't have another chance for a while. We'll be in St Tropez for most of next week, preparing for the launch of the new Di Cosimo restaurant, and after that I plan to spend some time in Positano.'

'I assume you'll want me to be here in Rome, to run the office while you are staying at your villa?' Gina murmured, trying not to dwell on how much she would miss him. He probably had a mistress in Positano, she thought bleakly, despising herself for the corrosive jealousy that burned like acid in her stomach.

'Of course not—I'll be working from the villa, and naturally I will require my personal assistant to be with me.'

Lanzo got to his feet and stared down at her, feeling his body stir into urgent life as his eyes were drawn to the deep valley between her breasts revealed by her low-cut vest top. After spending all week fantasising about the voluptuous curves she kept hidden beneath smart work suits and high-necked blouses, the sight of her in denim shorts and the clingy lemon yellow top at breakfast this morning had sent heat surging through his veins.

He could not remember ever wanting a woman as badly as he wanted Gina, he acknowledged, almost resenting her for the hold she seemed to have over him. He had told himself he would wait until she accepted that their mutual attraction could only have one inevitable conclusion, but he hadn't reckoned on her ability to shatter his peace of mind.

Lanzo took Gina's hand and drew her to her feet, but instead of leading her out of the courtyard he stood towering over her, so that she was faced with the choice of staring at his muscle-bound chest, and the tantalising glimpse of tanned flesh above the neckline of his shirt, or the chiselled perfection of his face.

'I want you to come to Positano with me,' he said, in

his rich-as-molten-chocolate voice that made the hairs on
the back of her neck stand on end. 'And not just as my PA,
cara.'

Her eyes flew to his, and she caught her breath at the
feral hunger gleaming in his green gaze. Tension quivered
between them, and the air in the courtyard was so still
and silent that Gina was sure he could hear the frantic
thud of her heart. 'You shouldn't say things like that,' she
whispered. He had broken the unspoken promise between
them—not to refer to their mutual awareness of each other—and she felt exposed and vulnerable.

'Why not—when it's the truth?' His arm snaked around
her waist and he jerked her up against him, so that she could
feel every muscle and sinew of his hard thighs pressing into
her softer flesh. 'You must know that I want you,' he said
roughly. 'And you want me too. Do you think I don't notice
the hungry glances you give me, or the way you trace your
lips with your tongue, inviting me to kiss you?'

'I don't—' Gina stopped dead, horrified to realise that
she had unconsciously moistened her lips with the tip of her
tongue even while Lanzo was speaking. But not because she
wanted him to kiss her, she assured herself. Not because
she longed for him to cover her mouth with his own and
plunder her very soul.

His dark head blotted out the sun, and her heart beat
faster as she saw the determined intent in his eyes. She
should move, she thought desperately, but her body would
not follow the dictates of her brain, and the soft brush of
his lips over hers opened the floodgates of desire that she
had tried so hard to deny.

Her common sense warned her not to respond, but already it was too late. She had no weapons to fight his sorcery. Her hands were shaking as she placed them against his
chest, intending to push him away. The trembling that now

affected all her limbs was not from fear, but from a fierce longing to press her body against the muscled strength of his and feel the thud of his heart echo the drumbeat of her own.

Lanzo tasted her again softly, carefully, as if he was aware that she was poised to flee from him. But the gentle pressure of his lips on hers tantalised her senses, and with a low moan she opened her mouth to welcome the erotic sweep of his tongue. And suddenly the dam broke, and he could no longer restrain the thundering torrent of his desire, kissing her with a blazing passion that had her clinging to him while he tangled his fingers in her long, silky hair.

It was Lanzo who finally broke the kiss, the functioning part of his brain reminding him that, although the little courtyard was deserted, they were in full view of the houses surrounding them. He lifted his head reluctantly and frowned. As the head of one of Italy's most successful companies he was a well-known figure in Rome. He never kissed his lovers in public, aware that paparazzi could be lurking anywhere. But yet again Gina had caused him to break one of his personal rules, he thought derisively.

He was unbearably tempted to take her back to his apartment and spend the afternoon making love to her, but once again the wariness in her eyes stopped him. He was sure now that some guy had hurt her in the past. She had brushed off his delicate attempts to probe into her romantic history, but her defensiveness told him there was a reason why she continued to pull back from him. Patience was a virtue, Lanzo reminded himself ruefully. Gina would be his soon, but he would not rush her.

'I leave it up to you to decide what we should do for the rest of the day, *cara*,' he murmured, forcing himself to ease away from her. 'We can go home and relax…' He paused, heat flaring inside him as he imagined removing her shorts and tee shirt and stroking his hands over her voluptuous curves. He took a ragged breath. 'Or we can visit the Pantheon, as we had planned to do.'

Gina stared at him in stunned silence, still reeling from his kiss. Part of her wished that he would make the choice for her, exert his dominance and whisk her back to his apartment so that he could take her to bed for the rest of the day. But she was afraid to admit her longing for him to make love to her. It was more than a step. It was a leap off a precipice. And her nerve failed her.

'I don't want an affair with you,' she said jerkily, cringing at her bluntness but needing to make it clear to him—to herself—that she was not in the market for a sexual fling.

His eyes narrowed, and she saw the effort he made to control his frustration. 'Why not?' he demanded. 'Don't think about denying the chemistry that burned between us when you responded to me so eagerly a few seconds ago. We were good together once,' he reminded her when she shook her head.

'Ten years ago you only wanted me for sex,' Gina reminded him shakily.

'That's not true.' It had started out like that, Lanzo admitted silently. He had been attracted to Gina, but he had assumed that once he had taken her to bed he would soon grow bored with her—as he did with all his mistresses. To his surprise his desire had increased with every week that they had been lovers. He had been drawn to her, and had wanted to spend all his time with her—until alarm bells had rung in his head and he had abruptly ended their affair, determined that he would never allow himself to become emotionally involved with any woman. He had learned that emotions hurt, and he was not prepared to risk going through the pain he had felt when he had lost Cristina ever again.

'It was not just sex. You meant something to me,' he said roughly.

'So much so that I never heard from you again after you returned to Italy?' Gina said bitterly. 'If you cared for me at all—' she could not believe he had '—why didn't you say so?'

'Because my head was messed up.' Lanzo exhaled heavily. 'I wasn't in a fit state of mind to contemplate a relationship. You were young and full of life. You deserved to meet a guy who would make you happy.'

Instead she had met Simon, Gina thought bleakly. 'Why was your head messed up?' she whispered. 'Sometimes I used to glimpse an almost haunted look in your eyes, but you never liked to talk about yourself.' She could tell from his shuttered face that things had not changed and he still would not confide in her. 'I never really knew you at all,' she said sadly. 'And now I don't want to spend a few more weeks as your convenient mistress.'

Lanzo stared at her intently. 'If I only wanted to satisfy a carnal urge there are any number of women I could call,' he said quietly. In truth he did not know exactly what he wanted from a relationship with Gina, but they had been friends as well as lovers ten years ago, and he saw no reason why they could not be so again now. His jaw tightened when he saw panic flare in her eyes. 'What are you afraid of, Gina?'

'I'm not…' The denial died in her throat when he gave her a look of frank disbelief.

'Does your nervousness stem from a previous relationship?' Lanzo voiced what he had begun to suspect, and knew he was near the mark when she quickly looked away from him.

'I don't want to talk about it,' she muttered, stubbornness creeping into her tone. As she pushed her hair back from her face Lanzo noted that her hand was shaking, and a feeling of tenderness swept through him.

'Maybe we both need to open up?' he suggested softly. He wanted to pull her close and simply hold her, until she felt with every beat of his heart that she could trust him. But as he moved towards her she stepped back and shook her head once more.

'What's the point? The only relationship I want with you is as your temporary PA.'

'Look me in the eye and tell me that,' Lanzo ordered, frustrated that he could not understand why she was determined not to give in to the chemistry that was a constant simmering presence between them.

Gina was glad that she had reached into her bag for her sunglasses. She slipped them on and met his gaze calmly, thankful that her expression was hidden from him. 'That's all I want,' she repeated firmly, desperately trying to convince herself as much as him, and before he could say another word she turned and walked out of the courtyard.

There was luxury, and then there was out-of-this-world breathtaking opulence, Gina thought as she stared around in awe at the new Di Cosimo restaurant in St Tropez. Nestled in the hills above the town, it offered diners spectacular views over the bay and the harbour, where huge yachts and motor cruisers—undoubtedly owned by the many multi-millionaires who flocked to the French Riviera during the summer—were moored.

The restaurant was all white marble floors and pillars, with wallpaper flecked with the kind of gold-leaf which also gilded the Louis XV style dining chairs and matched the gold cutlery set out on pristine white linen tablecloths. Stunning centrepieces of white calla lilies and orchids filled the air with their heavenly fragrance, adding to the restaurant's ambience of sumptuous elegance.

'Are you impressed?' Lanzo's deep voice sounded from behind her and she spun round, her breath catching in her throat at the sight of him looking breathtakingly handsome in a formal black dinner suit.

'I'm speechless,' she replied honestly. 'The décor is amazing. And the view from the terrace—those bright pink bougainvillea bushes and beyond them the sapphire-blue sea—is wonderful. I've never seen anything so beautiful.'

'I agree,' Lanzo said softly, not glancing at the view out of the window. Instead his eyes were fixed intently on Gina as he made a slow appraisal of her heather-coloured silk-chiffon dress. Floor-length and strapless, the dress clung to her curves and emphasised her slender waist. She had piled her hair into a chignon with soft tendrils left loose to frame her face, and her only adornment was the rope of pearls that had once been her grandmother's. The smooth, luminescent stones were displayed perfectly against her creamy skin.

'The view from where I'm standing is exquisite,' he murmured, watching dispassionately as soft colour flared along her cheekbones. Since he had kissed her in Rome their relationship had shifted subtly, and the tension between them was tangible. For the past week that they had been in St Tropez, Gina had been excruciatingly polite towards him, perhaps afraid that if they reverted to the easy friendliness they had shared since she had begun to work for him he would think she was willing to have an affair with him.

But despite her coolness Lanzo had been conscious of the fierce sexual chemistry bubbling beneath the surface, waiting to explode. He felt strung out and edgy, his body in a permanent state of arousal—and his patience was at an end. His concentration was shot to pieces, his thoughts dominated by his need to take Gina to bed, and he knew from the way her eyes darkened every time she looked at him that her longing was as great as his.

'Yes, well, everything is ready for the grand opening,' Gina said shakily, dragging her eyes from Lanzo's glinting gaze to glance at her watch. Her senses quivered as she inhaled the subtle scent of his cologne and she took a step away from him, terrified that he would notice her body's betraying reaction to him, her nipples jutting beneath the sheer silk of her gown. 'The guests should start to arrive soon.'

She had barely uttered the words when a sleek black limousine drew up outside the restaurant and moments later a well-known Hollywood star emerged from the car.

The guest list for tonight was chock-full of celebrities, and no expense had been spared to make the launch of the latest Di Cosimo restaurant an event that would hit the headlines around the world. Luisa had begun to organise the launch party before she had gone on maternity leave, but Gina had spent a hectic week finalising arrangements and dealing with last minute problems. Added to that, she had endured four days of the usual agony that accompanied her monthly period. She knew that the painful stomach cramps were a sign that her endometriosis was getting worse, and she was filled with an unbearable sadness that she was unlikely to ever have children.

The only good thing was that she had been so tired and drained at the end of each day that she hadn't had much time to think about Lanzo—although it had been difficult to ignore the escalating sexual tension between them. She did not know what to make of his assertion that he wanted her for more than just sex. If he did not want her for his mistress, what *did* he want? she wondered fretfully. She wished she had the courage to find out, but her marriage and subsequent divorce from Simon had been a bruising experience—and not just mentally, she thought ruefully, her hand straying unconsciously to the scar she had skilfully disguised with make-up. She was afraid to trust her judgement, afraid to give her trust to Lanzo, and now they seemed to be trapped in a strange stalemate which was dominated by their desperate physical awareness of each other.

She was dragged from her thoughts when Lanzo drew her arm through his. 'Duty time,' he murmured when her eyes flew to his face. 'We'll wait at the front entrance to greet the guests as they arrive.'

'Oh, but I thought that as you are the chairman of Di Cosimo Holdings you would prefer to do that on your own. Are you sure you want me...?' Gina trailed to a halt as he gave her an amused smile.

'I'm absolutely certain that I want you, *cara*,' he drawled, his eyes glinting when she blushed scarlet.

The launch party had been a great success, Gina mused hours later, stifling a yawn as she glanced at her watch and saw that it was almost midnight. The food had been divine, accompanied by a selection of the finest wines, and after dinner everyone had strolled out onto the terrace to enjoy the view and the endless supply of champagne served by white-jacketed waiters who wove through the throng of guests.

Inevitably some people had drunk too much—notably an English celebrity television presenter, who regularly featured in the gossip columns and was renowned for his rowdy behaviour. Finn O'Connell had grown increasingly brash and loud-mouthed as the evening progressed. He was swaying unsteadily on his feet, Gina noted, looking over to where Finn was standing with a group of people, including his pretty young wife. Miranda O'Connell was a talented stage actress, and like many people Gina wondered what she saw in her boorish husband.

Gina watched as Finn called to a waiter and demanded another glass of whisky—clearly he had moved on from champagne to neat spirits. His wife put her hand on his arm, as if to plead with him not to have another drink, and Finn reacted explosively, pushing Miranda away with such violence that she stumbled and fell. Gina heard the smash of glass on the tiled floor. As if in slow motion she saw Miranda fall, and memories instantly flooded her mind.

Dear heaven, no—not again, she thought as she flew across the terrace. She pictured Miranda landing on the broken glass, and it brought back the horror of feeling blood pouring in a hot, sticky stream down her own face. Finn O'Connell was shouting at the two burly security guards who had appeared out of the shadows and were gripping his arms. His wife was lying on the floor amid the shards of a broken glass, and Gina could barely bring herself to look, sure that Miranda must have been cut.

Lanzo got there first. He knelt by Miranda's side and spoke to her in a low tone before he gently helped her to her feet. There was no blood, Gina realised with relief. The young actress looked pale and shaken, but seemed otherwise unhurt.

'Stay with Mrs O'Connell while I arrange for a car to take her and her husband back to their hotel,' Lanzo instructed, glancing briefly at Gina. 'I'll tell a waiter to bring her some water—and black coffee for O'Connell,' he added grimly. 'He needs something to sober him up.'

'I'm fine, really,' Miranda said faintly as Lanzo strode away and Gina guided her to a chair. She bit her lip. 'Finn just gets carried away sometimes.'

'Fairly often, if the stories in the tabloids are even half right,' Gina said quietly. When Miranda did not refute this she murmured, 'You're not responsible for the fact that your husband drinks too much. And he has no excuse for lashing out at you—certainly not that he's downed too much whisky.'

Miranda gave her a startled look. 'You sound as though you're speaking from experience.'

Gina nodded. 'I am. Alcohol affects people in different ways; some become happy and relaxed, while others feel morose. My ex-husband used to become bad-tempered and aggressive.' She looked steadily at Miranda. 'I pleaded with Simon to seek help, but he refused to admit he had a problem. When his heavy drinking made him violent I knew that for my safety I had to leave him.' She hesitated, and gave the younger woman a sympathetic smile. 'It's not up to me to tell you how to live your life, but you need to take care of yourself—'

She broke off when Lanzo returned. 'Your car is waiting out front,' he told Miranda. 'I've taken the liberty of sending your husband back to your hotel in a separate car, accompanied by two of my staff. He seems more in control of himself now.' He did not add that Finn O'Connell's bravado had quickly dispersed when he had found himself sharing a car with the two burly bodyguards.

'I hope she'll be okay,' Gina murmured as she and Lanzo watched the hotel manager escort Miranda out of the restaurant.

'The security guards will make sure O'Connell behaves himself for the rest of tonight. Anyway, he's so drunk that he's probably out cold by now. Not that that's an excuse. Any man who hits a woman is a pathetic coward,' Lanzo said disgustedly. He glanced at Gina and frowned. 'Are you all right? You're deathly pale.'

'I'm tired. It's been a long day,' she said hurriedly, desperate to deflect any further questions.

'Go back to the hotel and get to bed. I'll call the driver to take you,' Lanzo said, taking his phone from his jacket. 'I have a few things to finish up here.'

She *was* weary—it hadn't just been an excuse, Gina realised. The upsetting events with Miranda and Finn had been the final straw, and so she did not argue, simply collected her shawl and allowed Lanzo to escort her out to his limousine.

They were staying just outside St Tropez, in a stunning five-star beach-front hotel. Some months ago Luisa had booked the luxurious Ambassador Suite for Lanzo, but she had not made arrangements for any staff who would be accompanying him. When Gina had later phoned the hotel to book a room for herself, and learned that there were no vacancies, she would have been happy to stay at another hotel. But Lanzo had insisted that she should share his suite.

'It has two bedrooms, each with *en suite* bathrooms, as well as an enormous lounge. It's ridiculous for you to stay somewhere else. After all, it won't be any different than us living together in my apartment in Rome,' he'd pointed out when she had tried to argue.

The gleam in Lanzo's eyes had warned Gina of his determination to have his own way, and from a work point of view sharing the suite made sense, she had been forced to admit. But tonight, as she crossed the spacious lounge and entered her bedroom, she locked the door behind her as she had done every night—although whether her actions were to keep Lanzo out or to stop herself from succumbing to temptation and going to him in the middle of the night, she refused to think about.

The night was hot and sultry, and from far out across the

bay came the distant rumble of thunder. Gina opened the French doors, hoping there would be a faint breeze blowing in from the sea, but the air was suffocatingly still.

The scene at the restaurant kept playing over in her mind, but she resolutely pushed it and all its associated memories away as she hung up her dress, washed off her make-up, and slipped a peach silk chemise over her head before she climbed into bed. She had been on her feet since six-thirty that morning, rushing around sorting out last-minute arrangements for the launch party, and she was grateful for the bone-deep weariness that swept over her so that sleep claimed her within minutes.

An hour later Lanzo entered the suite and made straight for the bar, where he poured himself a large brandy. It was his first drink of the night, for although the guests at the party had enjoyed unlimited champagne, he never drank alcohol while he was representing Di Cosimo Holdings. Nursing his glass, he strolled over to the French doors and opened them to step out onto the terrace. The sky was black, lit by neither moon nor stars, and the air prickled with an electricity that warned of an imminent storm.

As he stared out across the dark sea, lightning suddenly seared the sky, ripping through the heavens and illuminating briefly the white wave-crests as they curled onto the shore. His jaw hardened. The day had been intolerably hot and sticky, and hopefully a downpour of rain would clear the air, but he hated storms.

It was ironic that there should be one tonight, he brooded grimly. He hardly needed a reminder that it had been on this date fifteen years ago that lightning had struck his parents' house in Positano and set it ablaze. The fire had been so intense and had spread so quickly that the occupants had not stood a chance. His parents and Cristina had been killed by smoke inhalation while they slept, and when the blaze had finally been brought under control the fire crew had found their bodies still in bed.

He lifted his glass and drained it, feeling the brandy forge a fiery path down his throat. He could no longer see Cristina's face clearly in his mind; time had shrouded her features behind its misty veil and it was now Gina's face, her sapphire-blue eyes and her mouth that tilted upwards at the corners, that was burned onto his brain.

The sound of a cry dragged him from his reverie. It had been a cry of terror—a sharp, frantic cry of mingled fear and pain—and it had come from Gina's room. Pausing only to set his glass down on the table, Lanzo strode swiftly along the terrace, while above him the heavens grumbled menacingly.

CHAPTER SIX

THERE was so much blood. It was hot and wet, pumping all over her white dress and already forming a pool around her head. Gina tossed restlessly beneath the sheet, lost in her dream. She was amazed that she had that much blood, but she needed to stop it pouring out.

With a cry, she jerked upright and pressed her hand to her cheek. It was dark, so dark that she couldn't see, but as the dream slowly ebbed she realised that she wasn't lying on the hard kitchen tiles, and there was no smashed glass beneath her face, no blood seeping from her.

With a shaking hand she fumbled for the switch on the bedside lamp, and at once a soft glow lit up the room. Gina drew a ragged breath. It was a long time since she'd had the dream, and she knew it had been triggered by the events in the restaurant earlier, when Finn O'Connell had pushed his wife and she had fallen, her wine glass shattering on the ground seconds before she had landed. Miranda hadn't been cut, thankfully. But the incident had brought back memories of Simon, drunk and aggressive, hitting her when she tried to take a bottle of whisky from him. The bottle had slipped to the floor, spilling its contents. The smell of whisky still made her feel sick.

Afterwards, Simon had insisted that he hadn't meant to hit her, but whether by accident or design his blow to her temple had been so hard that she had reeled and fallen. She'd been shocked, and she hadn't had time to put out her hands. She had landed on the broken glass, which had sliced through her face and neck.

Pushing back the sheet, she jumped out of bed and fumbled to the open French doors, needing to escape the hot, dark room and the suffocating blackness of her dream. There was no moonlight, and she screamed when she walked into something solid. Hands gripped her arms as she lashed out.

'Gina!' Lanzo spoke her name urgently, shocked by her haunted expression. 'What's the matter, *cara*?'

It was the *cara* that undid her. Lanzo's voice was deep and soft, strength and gentleness meshed, so that she felt instantly safe. She felt instinctively that he would rather die than cause a woman physical harm. He was man of surprisingly old-fashioned values, who opened doors and gave up his seat, and considered it a man's role to protect the weaker sex. Female emancipation was all very well, but at this moment, when she was trembling and felt sick inside, Gina simply allowed him to draw her close and stood silently while he stroked his hand through her hair.

'What happened?' he asked gently.

'Nothing…I had a nightmare, that's all,' she whispered, unable to restrain a shiver as she recalled the details of the dream.

Lanzo gave her a searching glance, feeling a curious little tug in his gut when he saw the shimmer of tears in her eyes. 'Want to talk about it?'

'No.' She swallowed, and tore her eyes from the unexpected tenderness in his.

He sighed and tightened his arms around her, resting his chin on top of her head. No way was he going to allow her to return to her bed alone when she was still clearly upset about her dream. He knew about nightmares. He still suffered from them himself sometimes: tortured images of Cristina, crying out for him amid the flames, and of him unable to save her. He knew what it was like to wake sweating and shaking, afraid to go back to sleep in case the nightmare came again, Lanzo thought grimly.

Gina's hair smelled of lemons. He could not resist the temptation to brush his mouth over her temple, smiling when she gave a jolt but did not try to pull away from him. Gently he trailed his lips down her cheek and over the faint ridge of her scar. She immediately tensed.

'Was your nightmare about the car crash?' he murmured.

Gina drew back a little and gave him a puzzled look. 'What car crash?'

'I assumed you were cut by glass from a shattered windscreen.' It was the only explanation he had been able to think of. 'How *were* you injured, then, *cara*?' He frowned, feeling the tension that gripped her body. Something came into his mind—an image of Gina's terrified face when she had witnessed the incident in the restaurant earlier that night. When Finn O'Connell had lashed out at his wife Gina had looked as shaken as Miranda O'Connell.

A horrific understanding slowly dawned on him. 'Did someone hurt you?' he demanded roughly, feeling sick inside at the possibility. 'Did somebody do this to you, *cara*?'

Gina bit her lip when Lanzo ran his finger lightly down her scar. The compassion evident in his eyes was too much when her nightmare about Simon's brutality was still so real in her head. She felt desperately vulnerable, and her primary instinct was to retreat mentally and physically from Lanzo.

He must have read her mind, for he slid his hand from

her scar to her nape, massaging her tight muscles with a gentle, repetitive motion. 'I would never harm you in any way, *cara*,' he said deeply. 'You must know that.'

She recalled the year she had dated Simon before their marriage, when she'd had no inkling that he had a drink problem and seen no sign of his violent temper. Her wedding night had been memorable for all the wrong reasons, she thought ruefully. Simon had seemed fine after a couple of glasses of champagne at the reception, but on the plane he had ordered spirits, and numerous shots of neat whisky had revealed a side to his personality that had come as an unwelcome shock.

How could you ever know a person's true nature? Gina wondered. And yet she felt safe with Lanzo. She trusted him. And as that realisation sank in relief seeped through her. She had feared she would never feel confident enough to trust anyone again, but Lanzo *was* different from Simon—so different that it was hard to believe they were of the same species.

Lanzo watched the play of emotions on Gina's face, the faint tremor of her mouth before she quickly compressed her lips, and felt a hard knot of anger form in his gut at the idea of some guy hurting her.

'What happened?' he asked quietly, smoothing her hair back from her face and catching her fingers in his when she instinctively tried to cover the thin, slightly raised ridge that he had exposed.

She was under no obligation to tell him anything—so why did she feel a strong urge to share the memories that still had the power to evoke nightmares? He was so tall that she had to tilt her head to look at his face, and as she studied his hard jaw a wry smile tugged her lips. Strength and undeniable power meshed with the gentle expression in his eyes were a potent combination. She felt safe with Lanzo; it was as simple as that.

But it was still hard to admit the truth. Gina took a shaky breath. 'My husband…did this,' she said huskily. 'He was in one of his rages and he hit me.'

For a few stark seconds Lanzo went rigid with shock. 'You're *married*?' he demanded harshly.

'Not any more.' She managed a ghost of a smile that did not reach her eyes. 'My divorce was finalised just before I moved back to Poole, but I *had* left Simon a year before that. The night he did this—' she touched her scar '—was the final straw. I knew I had to get away from him before anything worse happened.'

'*Dio mio,*' Lanzo growled. 'How on earth did you end up married to such a monster in the first place?'

Gina bit her lip. It was a question that the few close friends who knew what had happed during her marriage had asked her. She felt a fool that she had been duped by Simon, and it was hard for her to talk about her marriage, but she acknowledged that she was never going to be able to move forward with her life until she had come to terms with her past.

'Simon was an investment banker. We met at a corporate dinner in the City,' she explained wearily. 'He was good-looking, charming, and successful—I guess he ticked all the right boxes, and we quickly became close. We were engaged six months after we met, and married six months after that. Our wedding night was the first time I had ever seen him drunk, but the next morning he was so apologetic that I put it down to the stress of the wedding.'

She sighed. 'Making excuses for Simon's drinking and his black moods became a regular occurrence, but I wanted our marriage to work and so I kept on ignoring the warning signs of his increasing reliance on alcohol.'

'I don't understand how you could have ignored it if he was violent towards you,' Lanzo said harshly. It struck him that Gina must have been madly in love with her husband to put up with his behaviour, and he was unprepared for the sharp stab of jealousy in his gut that the thought evoked.

Gina could see the shock in Lanzo's eyes and she hung her head, moving away from him to stare out of the window at the dark beach. 'I was ashamed,' she admitted in a low tone. 'I thought that I must somehow be to blame for Simon's drinking and his tempers. And I didn't know who to talk to. We were part of a large social group, but most of the people we met at dinner parties were Simon's business associates and I couldn't possibly have confided to any of them or their sophisticated wives that we were not the glamorous have-it-all couple we appeared to be.'

She twisted her fingers together, still not able to look at Lanzo. 'I know I was a fool, but I was clinging to my dream of having a family. We had agreed to try for a child as soon as we were married, and I hoped that a baby would magically make Simon stop drinking. Instead, I failed to fall pregnant, Simon lost his job in the banking crisis that hit the City, and things went rapidly from bad to awful because he spent all day at home drowning his sorrows.'

'Yet you still stayed with him?'

'I wanted to help him. I felt guilty that I didn't love the man he had turned into, but I was still his wife, and I felt it was my duty to try and support him. The trouble was Simon didn't want to be helped. During one of our many rows about his drinking I tried to take his bottle of whisky, and he reacted like a madman.' She swallowed, the memories vivid in her mind. 'He struck me, and as I fell I dropped the bottle I was holding. A piece of broken glass sliced through my face, and by unlucky chance through an artery in my neck. There was a lot of blood and confusion.

I needed numerous stitches, and was left with this lasting reminder of my marriage,' she said wryly, lifting her hand to trace the familiar path of her scar.'

'No wonder you looked so ashen when Finn O'Connell turned on his wife tonight,' Lanzo said harshly, feeling a fierce need to search out Gina's ex and connect his fist with the other man's face.

He noticed the glimmer of tears in her eyes and his gut clenched. Giving in to his own violent urges where her ex-husband was concerned would not help her, he acknowledged grimly. He sensed that it had taken enormous bravery for her to tell him about her marriage, and now she needed his support and strength. Suppressing his inner rage against her ex, he walked over to her and drew her into his arms.

'You were not to blame for your husband's drink problem any more than Miranda is responsible for O'Connell's behaviour,' he assured her firmly.

He bent his head and brushed his lips the length of her scar, the caress as soft as thistledown, causing a curious little pain in Gina's heart. He's simply being kind, she told herself sternly. Don't read more into it than that. She knew she should pull away from him, assure him that she had recovered from the nightmare and would be able to sleep now. Except that was a lie; she doubted she could fall asleep—not because of the bad memories of Simon, which were fading as the nightmare receded, but because of other memories, of Lanzo drawing her down onto the soft grass in that wooded glade many years ago, and making love to her with exquisite gentleness.

She swallowed when he lifted his head and stared down at her. Desire was still evident in his green gaze, but it was tempered with compassion and understanding, an unspoken vow that she was safe with him.

She sighed and felt the tension drain out of her, so that

she relaxed in his arms. Perhaps it was the knowledge that Lanzo would never hurt her as Simon had done, or the memory of his gentle caresses the first time he had made love to her all those years ago when she had been a girl on the brink of womanhood. Or perhaps it was simply that she could not deny her need for him any longer—a need that was mirrored in his hypnotic green eyes. All she knew was that when he slowly lowered his head she *ached* for him to kiss her, and instead of pulling away from him she parted her lips in readiness, her heart thudding with excitement rather than fear as he brushed his mouth lightly over hers.

Lanzo felt the tremor that ran through her, and was shocked to realise that it was not only Gina who was shaking. This moment had been building since he had first caught sight of her in Poole. He had known immediately that he wanted her, and a little later, when he had realised her identity—that she was *his* Gina, who had been his lover ten years before—his desire for her had intensified. He had not known then of the trauma she had suffered at the hands of her ex-husband, and now his desire was mingled with a need to show her that he would only ever treat her with the greatest care and respect.

He did not want to rush her. He wanted to savour every second, every soft sigh that whispered from Gina's lips as he drew her closer and deepened the kiss so that it became a sensual tasting that was both evocative and erotic.

Gina was aware of Lanzo's powerful arousal jutting against her pelvis, and she felt the drenching flood of desire between her legs. By choice she hadn't had a physical relationship with a man since her marriage had ended, but she was sure now that she wanted Lanzo to make love to her and obliterate the dark memories of Simon that still haunted her.

She knew she was risking her heart. Lanzo had ended their affair ten years ago, and from all that she had read about him since he still had an aversion to commitment. But nothing altered the fact that she wanted him. She yearned to feel his hands sliding over her naked body, the brush of his hair-roughened thighs pressing against her softer flesh. Dear heaven, the sensual tug of his mouth on her breast.

It was impossible to express her need in words, so she captured his face between her palms and drew his mouth down to hers, to kiss him with an unrestrained hunger that made him groan deep in his throat.

Passion exploded between them: wild, almost pagan in its intensity, and leaving no room for doubt. Without taking his lips from hers, Lanzo swept Gina up and carried her along the terrace to where the door to his bedroom stood ajar. He stepped inside and paused, looking down at her for long minutes, searching for an answer to his unspoken question before he gently lowered her onto the bed.

'You are so beautiful, *tesoro*,' he said thickly, his accent very pronounced. 'I swear I would never do anything to harm you.'

He dropped down next to her and threaded his fingers through her hair, which was spread like a curtain of chestnut-coloured silk around her shoulders. Tiny buttons secured the front of her chemise, and Gina snatched a breath when he deftly unfastened them and then slowly drew the thin straps down her arms until he had bared her breasts.

The air felt cool on her heated skin. She felt a dragging sensation low in her stomach when he stilled and allowed his gaze to roam over the creamy mounds of firm flesh that he had exposed, dark colour winging along his cheekbones, his eyes glittering with feral desire.

He leaned forward and slanted his mouth over hers, kissing her with a slow deliberation that could not disguise his barely leashed hunger. Only when her lips were softly swollen did he move his head lower, trailing a moist path down to her collarbone and then over the slopes of her breasts. Her nipples tautened in anticipation of his caress, her heart thudding, and she gave a little moan when he flicked his tongue delicately across one rosy crest and then its twin, back and forth, heightening her pleasure to fever-pitch until she curled her fingers in his hair and held him to her breast, sighing her approval when he sucked hard, sending starbursts of sensation shooting down to her pelvis.

This was where she wanted to be, Gina thought dreamily, watching through heavy-lidded eyes as Lanzo stripped off his shirt. His chest gleamed like polished bronze in the lamplight, his powerful abdominal muscles clearly defined beneath the whorls of dark hair that arrowed down over his flat stomach. He stood to remove his trousers, and she felt a mixture of excitement and trepidation when his boxers hit the floor and he stood before her, gloriously and unashamedly aroused.

He must have misinterpreted her expression, for he said fiercely, 'You want me, *cara*. Your body reveals what you might wish to deny—see…?' he murmured, as he cupped her breasts in his palms and rolled her nipples between his fingers until she gasped and arched her hips in frantic invitation.

'I don't deny it,' she choked with innate honesty, her eyes widening when he skimmed his lips over her stomach and gently pushed her thighs apart. 'Lanzo…' Shock drove words of protest from her mind as he stroked his tongue lightly up and down the opening of her vagina, the sensation so exquisite that she instinctively spread her legs a little wider and groaned when he discovered the tight nub of her clitoris.

Pleasure was building inside her, coiling, tightening,

until she was trembling and desperate for his ultimate possession.

'I know, *cara*,' he growled, his voice rough with need as he moved over her, his body tense and his erection rock-hard. With one hand he tugged the chemise down over her hips and settled himself between her thighs, supporting his weight on his forearms. Gina slid her arms around his back and urged him down onto her, desperate to feel him deep inside her, but suddenly he stilled and muttered an imprecation.

'What's wrong…?' she whispered shakily.

Lanzo cursed again and shook his head. 'I don't have anything with me,' he gritted, struggling to control his body's urgent clamour to sink his throbbing shaft into her. 'Condoms,' he elucidated when she stared at him uncomprehendingly. 'I hadn't planned on this happening—at least not tonight,' he added wryly, 'and I didn't buy any contraception.' He gave an agonised groan, 'I'm sorry, *cara*, but even in the heat of passion I'm sure that neither of us is prepared to risk an accidental pregnancy.'

A shudder of longing ripped through Gina. Still haunted by memories of how Simon had treated her, it had taken a great deal of courage for her to get this far. But Lanzo's gentleness had given her the confidence to lower her barriers, and she was desperate to make love with him and prove to herself that she was no longer affected by her marriage. Driven by instinct, she gripped his shoulders to prevent him from rolling away from her.

'There's no risk,' she muttered.

Lanzo frowned, his heart kicking against his ribs as fierce excitement quickly mounted. 'You mean you are protected?' he demanded, assuming that she meant she was on the pill. Never before had he broken his golden rule and had sex without taking responsibility for contraception, but the pill was regarded as the most reliable method available, his brain argued, and he could not bear another night of aching, agonising frustration. It was not only about sex, he realised. He wanted to obliterate Gina's memories of her violent ex-husband, and remind her that the passion they had once shared had not faded.

'Gina...?' he said urgently, his body shaking with his desire to ensure her pleasure. He sensed that it had been a long time since she had enjoyed making love in its true sense—a sensual experience shared by two people totally in tune with each other's needs.

Gina wondered if she should reassure Lanzo that the chances of her falling pregnant were non-existent. Not only was her endometriosis worse, but her period had only just finished, and she knew from all the months she had obsessively studied her ovulation chart, when she and Simon had been trying for a baby, that her one minuscule chance of conceiving was around the middle of her cycle.

But she did not want to discuss her infertility; she didn't want to waste time talking when her body was trembling with an intense yearning to take him inside her. The feel of his solid erection jabbing into her belly drove every consideration from her mind but her need to assuage the agonising, aching longing for him to possess her.

She touched the hard line of his jaw and traced her finger lightly over his mouth. 'I want you to make love to me, Lanzo,' she whispered, and heard his feral groan as he crushed her mouth beneath his in a possessive kiss. She felt his hand slip between her thighs and squirmed at the intimate probing of his finger as he parted her and stroked her until she was on the brink. 'Please...'

It was a cry from the heart, and he gave a rough laugh as he positioned himself above her.

'I intend to please you, *cara*,' he assured her. He could

feel that he was going to come at any second, but with a massive effort of will he controlled himself and gently eased forward, entering her carefully and oh, so slowly, pausing while her muscles stretched to accommodate him. He slid his hands beneath her and cupped her bottom, angling her so that it was easier for her to absorb his length, smiling down at her when she stared at him with stunned eyes. 'Good?' he queried softly.

Good did not come anywhere near it. There were no words to describe the intensity of pleasure that was beginning to build deep inside her as Lanzo withdrew a little and then drove into her, setting a rhythm that she eagerly matched. She clung to his shoulders, her lashes drifting down as she was swept away to a place where sensation ruled. Little spasms rippled across her belly as he increased his pace. She sensed his urgency and gasped his name, wanting the journey never to end. But the coiling inside her was growing ever tighter, and suddenly, cataclysmically, it snapped, and her cries of pleasure were muffled by his lips as he thrust his tongue into her mouth in erotic mimicry of the powerful thrusts of his body.

Lanzo could not hold back. The pleasure of feeling her body convulse around his throbbing shaft was too exquisite to bear, and he climaxed seconds after her, tensing for a few seconds as he tried to hold back the tide before he was overwhelmed, and then shuddering with the mind-blowing intensity of his release.

For long moments they lay, still joined, their mutual urgent need appeased for now, their bodies relaxing in the honeyed afterglow of lovemaking. It had never been like this with Simon—not even in those early days of their marriage when she had been sure that she loved him, Gina brooded. She had only ever felt this complete union, as if their souls as well as their bodies were one, with Lanzo.

But she did not kid herself that he felt the same way. He was a skilled and considerate lover who had taken her to the heights of ecstasy, but now, as he rolled off her, she sensed that his withdrawal was not only physical.

Should she get up and go back to her own bed? she wondered as she lay next to him, the silence between them broken by the sound of heavy rain lashing the windows. Some time during their frantic lovemaking the storm outside had broken, but she had been so swept away by passion that she had not even noticed. She pushed back the sheet, but as she eased away from him he curved his arm around her waist and pulled her up against his chest.

'Where are you going?' he growled, nuzzling the sensitive spot behind her ear so that she could not restrain a little shiver of pleasure.

'I was going to return to my room.'

Her answer should have pleased him, Lanzo brooded. He rarely spent the whole night with his lovers for once his physical needs had been satisfied he had no further need of them.

Through the open curtains the black sky was suddenly lit up by a jagged lightning bolt, and seconds later a deep rumble of thunder reverberated around the room, drowning briefly the sound of torrential rain. The storm had faded for a while, but now it was back to vent the full force of its fury.

The fire that had destroyed his parents' villa had raged out of control long before the rain had finally fallen during that devastating storm fifteen years ago. Perhaps if the heavens had opened as dramatically they had done tonight the flames might have been quenched and his parents and Cristina would have escaped, Lanzo thought heavily.

He did not want to be alone with his thoughts tonight. Ten years ago he had found solace and a few weeks of unexpected happiness with a shy young English waitress. He had never spoken to Gina about his past, but her gentle nature had soothed his ragged emotions, and when they had made love he had delighted in her unrestrained pleasure. Gina had made him forget briefly the pain inside him— and tonight he wanted to lie in her arms and focus on her silken skin and her soft, curvaceous body.

She had her own demons, too. Raw anger flared inside him as he thought of her brutal ex-husband. The fact that Simon had been an alcoholic did not excuse his behaviour, Lanzo thought savagely. He could not dismiss the image of her terrified face when she had stumbled into his arms, the horrors of her nightmare clearly evident in her eyes. He could not allow her to return to her room and perhaps be plagued once more by bad dreams. He wanted to hold her so that she felt safe for the rest of the night.

'Stay,' he murmured, trapping her against him by hooking his thigh over hers. Her bottom felt delightfully soft beneath his fingertips as he traced its rounded contours, before sliding his hands up to cup her breasts, and he heard her swiftly indrawn breath when he gently played with her nipples. He trailed one hand down over her flat stomach and slipped it between her thighs.

'Lanzo…?'

He ignored her breathless protest and carefully parted her womanhood, sliding his fingers between the slick folds and caressing her with delicate strokes that made her gasp and move restlessly against him.

'This is all for you, *cara*,' he whispered in her ear, when she attempted to turn round so that he could enter her.

Gina gave a little cry of pleasure when his clever fingers found her ultra-sensitive clitoris. She wanted him to share the experience, but he seemed determined to give her the ultimate in sexual enjoyment while unselfishly denying himself. The pleasure was too intense to withstand, and she sobbed his name as he took her to the edge, held her there, teetering on the brink, and then with a final stroke sent her tumbling over, holding her secure in his arms.

Afterwards he rearranged the pillows and settled her comfortably against him, feeling a curious tug on his heart when she gave him a sleepy smile.

'I imagine your experience with Simon has put you off marriage for good?' he murmured, unable to get the other man out of his mind.

Gina did not answer him straight away. She thought seriously about Lanzo's question. And discovered in those moments of contemplation that her hopes and dreams were still the same as when she had been eighteen.

'No,' she replied at last. 'My relationship with Simon was a disaster, but I still believe in marriage. I still hope that one day I'll meet the right person for me, just as Nonna Ginevra met my grandfather, and fall in love and marry again.' Her voice faltered a little. 'Have a family...' Maybe she would not be able have a baby of her own, but there were thousands of children who needed parents, and she would definitely consider adoption.

'I believe that just because something didn't go the way you planned it once, it's no reason not to try again,' she told Lanzo.

The expression in his green eyes was unfathomable. 'So you aren't afraid of having your heart broken again?'

By the time she had left Simon he had killed all her feeling for him, and the only emotion she had felt was relief that her marriage was over. There was only one man who had ever broken her heart, but wild horses would not drag the truth from her that that man had been Lanzo.

'Of course there's a risk that that could happen, but what is the alternative? To never allow myself to get close to anyone ever again? Never know the joy of loving someone for fear that it could end in tears? My heart might stay safe, but it wouldn't be much of a life.'

She paused, and then asked diffidently, 'Are you really content with *your* life, Lanzo? I know you have plenty of affairs, and technically you are never on your own when there is always another attractive blonde willing to share your bed, but I sense that you are alone,' she said softly. 'You don't seem to care about anyone.'

Lanzo had stiffened while she was speaking. There was a good reason why he refused to allow himself to get too close to anyone, he brooded. He remembered the savage pain that had ripped through him when he had been told that Cristina was dead—the disbelief that had turned to gut-wrenching agony when he had stared at the charred remains of his parents' house and realised that no one could have escaped such carnage. He never wanted to feel that kind of pain again, or sink to such depths of despair as he had in the months after the fire, when he had seriously wondered whether life was worth living without the woman he had loved. Fifteen years on he had forged a new life, and for the most part it was good. But he did not want to fall in love again.

'I like my life the way it is,' he admitted. 'I go where I please, when I please, and I answer to no one.'

He had not told her anything she did not already know, Gina acknowledged, trying to ignore the little pang his words had evoked. She had always known that Lanzo was essentially a loner—a man perfectly at ease in a crowd, but equally content with his own company.

How long would their affair last? A week? Months? she wondered, trying not to dwell on the inevitability of its ending.

She felt the need to take some control. Once his usual

PA returned to work, their professional *and* personal relationship would come to an end, she vowed. Their relationship could never be more than a brief interlude, and as long as she guarded her heart against him she would be content with that, she assured herself. For now she would enjoy every moment she spent with him, and she smiled as he drew her close and she felt the soft brush of his lips on hers.

CHAPTER SEVEN

THEY extended their stay in St Tropez for a few more days, spending lazy hours on the beach, and long nights of passionate lovemaking before falling asleep in each other's arms. Even in the early days of her marriage she had never felt this sense of completeness, Gina thought when she woke before Lanzo one morning, and lay studying his face. It seemed softer in sleep, reminding her of the younger man she had known ten years ago. Unable to resist, she leaned over him and brushed her mouth softly over his, stirring him so that he closed his arms around her and deepened the kiss into an evocative caress that tugged on her soul.

But it was not long before reality intruded. Lanzo's intention to fly back to Italy, to his home in Positano, was dramatically changed by news that the Di Cosimo restaurant in New York had been badly damaged by a fire.

'Arrange for the jet to collect us from Toulon-Hyres airport and take us direct to JFK,' he instructed Gina, after he had relayed the information he had received in a phone call from the manager of the restaurant.

'Has the restaurant been badly damaged?' she asked, remembering that the New York branch had recently undergone a major refit.

'I understand it's been gutted.' Lanzo shrugged. 'But

thankfully no one was injured in the blaze, and that's all that matters.'

Twenty-four hours after the fire, Gina stared around at the blackened walls and roof beams of the restaurant and shivered, despite the midday heat in New York. The fire had been caused by an electrical fault, and the damage was extensive—but, as Lanzo had said, thankfully every one of the diners and staff had escaped safely.

'Daniel Carter said he couldn't believe how quickly the flames took hold,' she said to Lanzo, after she had chatted with the restaurant manager who was clearly still in shock.

She glanced at him when he made no reply. From the moment they had arrived at what remained of the restaurant his expression had been unfathomable, but now he removed his sunglasses and she was shaken by the bleakness in his eyes.

'Fire is so appallingly destructive,' he said harshly. 'It consumes everything in its path and shows no mercy as it reduces everything to this.' As he spoke he kicked a pile of black ash, seemingly uncaring that his actions sent a cloud of choking soot into the air which fell back down and settled on his clothes.

Frowning at his obvious tension, Gina placed her hand on his arm. 'I know it's a terrible shame, but one of the fire crew told me that there is little actual structural damage, and although it looks like Armageddon the restaurant can be cleaned and redecorated.'

He gave a curious laugh. 'Sure—everything will be made shiny and bright again, and it will be as if the fire never happened.'

'Well, that would be good, wouldn't it?' she said slowly, trying to assess his mood. 'Six months from now the fire will be forgotten.'

Lanzo shook his head and moved away from her, so that her hand fell helplessly to her side. 'Some things can never be forgotten,' he muttered obliquely. 'Some memories haunt you for ever.'

'What do you mean?'

'It doesn't matter.' He swung to face her, his sunglasses back in place so that she had no clue to his thoughts. He seemed to give himself a mental shake and smiled at her, although she sensed that the smile did not reach his eyes. 'I'm talking rubbish, *cara*. It was just a shock to see how much damage the fire has caused. We'll go back to the hotel now. You must be feeling jet-lagged.'

Maybe Lanzo *was* feeling the effects of their frantic dash to the US and the six-hour time difference, Gina mused that night, when for the first time since they had become lovers he did not reach for her, but simply bade her goodnight and rolled onto his side of the vast hotel bed.

He was distant and preoccupied for the next few days, and when he did make love to her again the sex was urgent, and as mind-blowing as ever, but it lacked the intimacy that she had felt between them in St Tropez.

He soon returned to his usual charismatic self, but she sensed an edge of darkness beneath his easy charm which reminded her of how he had been when he had come to Poole ten years ago. Not for the first time she suspected that there were events in his past that he did not want to talk about.

They remained in New York for two weeks, while Lanzo dealt with the after-effects of the fire. On the Sunday before they were due to leave, Gina woke to find that he was already up and dressed.

'I'm spending the day out of town—a little place about sixty miles east of the city, near to the coast. Do you want to come?'

She pushed her hair out of her eyes and looked at him blearily, wondering how he could be so wide awake after a night of energetic sex and very little sleep. 'Okay.' It was stiflingly hot in town, and she liked the idea of a cool coastal breeze. 'When do you want to leave?'

'Twenty minutes.' He grinned at her dismayed expression. 'But I suppose that, seeing as I kept you busy for much of the night, I can give you half an hour.'

Two hours later Gina glanced around the flat airfield and then back at Lanzo. 'You seriously mean you've come here to *skydive*?'

'Certainly, *cara*,' he replied, looking amused at her horrified expression. 'Nothing beats throwing yourself out of a plane at ten thousand feet. I'm an experienced skydiver, and I can take you for a tandem jump if you like.'

'I'll give it a miss, thanks. I value my life.' She removed her sunglasses and gave him a searching look. 'Powerboat racing, skydiving, that super-powered motorbike you were telling me you keep in Positano—sometimes I get the feeling that you don't value yours, Lanzo.'

His own shades were firmly in place, disguising his thoughts, and he shrugged laconically. 'Life is more fun when it contains an element of risk, and I don't fear death.'

'No...' She sensed that was true. 'What you fear is allowing anyone to get too close.' She was frustrated that she only knew the man he allowed her to see, and that he never revealed his innermost thoughts to her. 'You don't mind risking your physical safety, but you refuse to put your emotional security in danger.'

She knew from the way his jaw tightened that she had pushed him too far. 'You don't know what I feel,' he said harshly. 'Do me a favour and keep your psychobabble to yourself, Gina,' he growled impatiently, and strode off towards the jump-plane waiting on the runway.

The following weeks were a hectic blur of planes, hotels, and occasionally brief trips to famous landmarks in whichever part of the world they happened to be in as they crisscrossed the globe, visiting various Di Cosimo restaurants and the new cookery schools which had proved to be a hugely successful project for the company.

Los Angeles, Dubai, Hong Kong, and Sydney blended into a kaleidoscope of images in Gina's head. She'd accompanied Lanzo to lavish parties, charity fundraising dinners, and the launch of his latest restaurant which had opened in Paris. Her previous job for the global retail outlet Meyers meant that she was no stranger to travel and socialising, and she was thankful that she had acquired a wardrobe of classic designer clothes which were now invaluable for her role as Lanzo's PA.

But while her smart work suits and elegant evening gowns were mainly from her days at Meyers, her nightwear was new—and bought for her by Lanzo. Skimpy lace negligees, delicate silk chemises, pretty bras, and matching thongs... Lanzo happily scoured lingerie shops for exotic and erotic underwear which he demanded that she model for him and then delighted in removing. Their desire for one another—far from waning as the weeks slipped past— was more intense than ever, and they made love with an insatiable hunger that left Gina secretly shocked by her unreserved response to Lanzo's bold demands.

And now at last they were in Positano, on the stunning Amalfi Coast, being driven by Lanzo's chauffeur along narrow roads with terrifying hairpin bends and spectacular views over an azure sea and the jagged rocky landscape.

Thank heavens Lanzo was not behind the wheel, Gina thought as she glanced out of the window at a hillside that fell in an almost sheer drop from the edge of the road down to the sea. She recalled those nerve-racking journeys in his car years ago, when he had driven her back to her father's farm after her she had finished her shift at the restaurant in Poole. If he were driving now they would no doubt be hurtling around the bends. Lanzo's love of danger had not changed, she thought ruefully. But their relationship was different from their brief affair when she had been eighteen; *she* was different—older, hopefully wiser, and determined that she would not give in to the clamour of her heart and fall in love with him again.

'It's so beautiful,' she murmured, awed by the picturesque view over the town. Dozens of terracotta-roofed houses clung to the cliffs which rose up majestically behind them, and in front of the houses the sea stretched into the far horizon, as flat and still as a lake, and crystal-clear.

'It's the most beautiful place in the world,' Lanzo agreed, his hard features softening a little as he drank in the familiar sights of the area where he had grown up. 'Around the next bend you will see my home—the Villa di Sussurri.'

'The villa of whispers,' Gina translated. 'Why is it called that?'

He looked away from her and stared at the sea, surprised by his strong urge to reveal that it was because he sometimes felt that he could hear the voices of his parents and Cristina in the house, speaking softly to him.

'No particular reason. I simply liked the name,' he said with a shrug.

'It's not what I was expecting,' Gina admitted a few minutes later, when the car swung onto a gravel driveway and halted outside the villa.

'You don't like it?'

'Oh, no—it's breathtaking,' she assured Lanzo hurriedly. 'I just assumed that it would be an old house, built of local stone, like the houses in Positano.' Instead the Villa di Sussurri was square and ultra-modern, built on several levels, its brilliant white walls making a stunning contrast to the vivid blue sky above and the sapphire sea below.

Lanzo ushered her into a cool marble-floored hall, and Gina caught her breath when he pushed open the double doors in front of them to reveal a huge lounge, with glass walls on all three sides offering spectacular views over the bay.

'Wow! This is stunning,' she murmured, glancing around at the pale walls and furnishings in muted shades of blue and taupe. Elegant and sophisticated, the villa managed to combine style with comfort, and it felt much homely than his apartment in Rome.

'This is my home,' he told her when she said as much. He smiled at her enthusiasm. 'Come on—I'll give you a guided tour.'

An open spiral stairway at one end of the villa led to the upper floors, where many windows allowed light to stream in, giving glimpses of the sea from almost every part of the house.

'It's huge; I've counted five bedrooms, and there's still another floor above us,' Gina commented. 'Don't you find it rather a big house for one person?'

'I'm not alone here very often,' he said carelessly.

'No…I don't suppose you are.' Her steps faltered, jealousy burning like acid in the pit of her stomach as she thought of all the other women he must have brought here, and all the others he would bring in the future, after she had been consigned to the metaphorical graveyard of his ex-mistresses.

Lanzo wondered if she knew how expressive her face was. Probably not, he mused. Gina went to great efforts to act cool with him—except for in bed, where she responded to him with gratifying eagerness. He skimmed his gaze over her, noting the expert cut of her cream skirt and jacket, which emphasised her gorgeous curves, and he felt the predictable tug of sexual anticipation in his groin.

'Most of the time Daphne is here to run the house for me,' he explained. 'Luisa stayed for a couple of weekends before she was married, when we had a lot of work to catch up on, but you are the only other woman I've invited to the villa, and the only woman to share my bed here,' he admitted.

As he spoke he opened a door, and stood back to allow Gina to precede him into what she saw instantly was the master bedroom. Decorated in the same neutral tones as the rest of the house, the room was airy and full of the evening sunlight which streamed through the huge windows, but it was the vast bed in the centre of the room that trapped her gaze, and a little frisson of excitement ran down her spine when Lanzo closed the door and pulled her into his arms.

'*Cara.*' His voice was as soft and sensuous as crushed velvet. When he slanted his mouth over hers she melted into his kiss, no thought in her head to deny him. This was where she wanted to be—in his arms and soon, she thought with a little shiver, in his bed.

She could not hide her disappointment when he lifted his head after a few moments and stared down at her. 'How are you feeling now, after your dizzy spell this morning?' he murmured, noting the faint shadows beneath her eyes. She had looked tired for the past couple of days, and had seemed a little subdued, but now she smiled up at him and traced her lips with the tip of her tongue in a deliberately provocative gesture that ignited the flame inside him.

'I'm fine. This morning was just…' She shrugged, not sure why she had felt so curiously light-headed when she had got out of bed the last few mornings. 'It was nothing.' She began to undo his shirt buttons, and skimmed her palm over the satiny skin overlaid with whorls of dark hair that she revealed. 'But perhaps I should have a lie-down?' she suggested huskily, smiling boldly at him as her deft fingers unzipped his trousers.

'Witch.' Lanzo gave a ragged laugh, his own fingers busy with her jacket buttons. 'All day I've wondered whether you were wearing a bra beneath your jacket. And now…' His eyes narrowed, hot, urgent desire pounding through his veins. 'Now I know that you are not.'

Dio, she turned him on. He shoved the jacket down her arms, so that it fell to the floor, and cupped her breasts in his hands, testing their weight and kneading the soft creamy globes before he lowered his head and took one pouting pink nipple into his mouth. Her soft moan of pleasure shattered the last remnants of his restraint and he tumbled them both down on the bed, thrusting his hand beneath her skirt and inside her knickers, to find the betraying dampness between her legs.

He could not have enough of her, he acknowledged as he stripped her with ruthless efficiency and tore off his own clothes, pausing briefly to don a protective sheath as he had done every time they had had sex after that first night in St Tropez. He was even thinking that it would not be a disaster if Luisa decided only to come back to work part-time after her maternity leave, as he suspected she was thinking of doing. He was confident that Gina would not need much persuading to remain his secretary-cum-mistress. It was an arrangement that could continue indefinitely, he mused, smiling as he drove into her with one long, deep thrust, and crushing her soft cry of delight beneath the hungry pressure of his mouth.

Afterwards he found himself reluctant to ease away from her, and when he finally rolled onto his back he drew her against him and idly stroked her hair, feeling a contentment that he had not known since... He tensed, shocked at the idea that he had not felt like this since he had made love to Cristina, so many years ago.

He glanced at Gina and saw that she had fallen asleep. Her long lashes lay against her flushed cheeks and her mouth was slightly parted, so that she looked young and curiously vulnerable. The feeling inside him was *not* the same, Lanzo told himself again. But he was no longer relaxed and, muttering a curse beneath his breath, he slid out of bed, taking care not to wake her, and strode into the *en suite* bathroom to take a shower.

Lanzo's housekeeper, Daphne, smiled warmly at Gina the following morning. '*Buongiorno*. Would you like to have your breakfast out on the terrace?'

The mere thought of food was enough to turn Gina's stomach, despite the fact that she hadn't eaten anything since lunch on the plane yesterday.

'Not just now, thank you.' She shook her head, trying to clear her muzzy thoughts. 'I can't believe I've slept for fifteen hours solid.'

'Lanzo said you have been working hard recently, and that it would be better to allow you to sleep for as long as you needed to,' Daphne explained. 'That's why he did not wake you for dinner last night. Are you sure you don't want something to eat now? You must be hungry.'

Gina wasn't. She felt horribly queasy. 'I'll have something in a while, when I've woken up properly. Where is Lanzo?'

'In the garden.' The housekeeper's smile faded. 'He spends many hours there, and he does not like to be disturbed.' She darted Gina a sharp look with her bright black eyes. 'But perhaps he will not mind you searching for him. Go through the gate in the wall at the side of the house.'

'Thank you.' Gina followed Daphne down the hall, pausing in front of the two life-sized portraits hanging on the wall. 'Are these people Lanzo's parents?' she asked as she studied the painting of a middle-aged couple, struck by the strong resemblance between the handsome square-jawed man and Lanzo. The woman at his side was dark haired and elegant, with a kindly smile that spoke of a warm nature.

'*Si.*' Daphne nodded, but offered no further information as she continued down the hall.

'And the young woman in the other painting—who is she?' Gina queried as the housekeeper opened a door and was about to step into the kitchen.

Was it her imagination, or did Daphne stiffen before she slowly turned around? 'She was Lanzo's *fidanzato*,' the older woman said expressionlessly.

Lanzo's *fiancée*! For a second Gina felt the walls and floor tilt alarmingly, just as had happened during the dizzy spell she had experienced when she had got out of bed that morning. Thankfully normality returned almost immediately, but she was conscious of a dull ache inside her at the startling news that Lanzo, who eschewed any form of emotional commitment, had once been *engaged*.

She stared at the portrait of the woman, and acknowledged that *beautiful* was nowhere near an adequate description of her exquisite features: huge almond-shaped eyes, a shy smile, and glossy black curls that fell around slender shoulders. A girl on the brink of womanhood, Gina mused, and felt a sharp stab to her heart as she wondered if Lanzo had loved her.

She frowned and turned back to Daphne. 'Where is she now? Why didn't Lanzo marry her?'

'She is dead.' The housekeeper finally looked at the paintings of Lanzo's parents and his fiancée. 'They are all dead. Lanzo does not like to speak of it,' she added grimly, before she disappeared into the kitchen.

Gina had noticed the high wall running next to the side of the villa when they had arrived yesterday, and now, as she stepped through the gateway, she found herself in an enclosed garden of such breathtaking beauty that she simply stood and stared around in amazement. Green lawns were edged with a profusion of colourful flowers, long walkways held climbing roses formed into a floral arbour, still pools showed goldfish darting beneath the surface, and the spray of fountains glinted in the sunshine like thousands of tiny diamonds. And all this with the backdrop of a sapphire sea, stretching away to the horizon where it met the cobalt blue sky.

If there was a heaven, this was what it would look like, she mused, her senses swamped by the sweet scent of the lavender bushes, where industrious bees buzzed among the long purple spires. The splash of the fountains was the only other sound to break the cloistered quiet, and Gina found herself breathing softly for fear of disturbing the peace and serenity that seemed to envelop her.

It was ten minutes before she found Lanzo. He was sitting on a low stone wall that surrounded a pool, watching the fish swim among the water lilies.

'Daphne told me you were here,' she greeted him, when he swung his head round and saw her hovering uncertainly beneath an archway of jasmine and orange blossom. 'She also said you might not wish to be disturbed—so if you want me to leave…?'

She wished she knew what he was thinking, but as usual his sunglasses hid his eyes. Yet she sensed that his mind was far away—perhaps with his beautiful fiancée? Her heart clenched and she despised herself for her jealousy. The beautiful girl in the portrait must have died tragically young—but of course she did not know, because Lanzo had never spoken of her.

He seemed to drag himself from a distant place and smiled at her. 'Of course I don't want you to leave. What do you think of my garden?'

'There aren't the words,' Gina said simply. 'Being here, surrounded by the flowers and trees, it's like a little piece of heaven on earth.'

She flushed, sure he would mock her, but he was quiet for a few moments.

'That's what I set out to create,' he said slowly. 'A beautiful paradise secluded from the hectic world. A place to reflect and perhaps find peace.'

Gina waited, unconsciously holding her breath as she wondered if he would speak of the girl in the painting, perhaps reveal how she and his parents had died. But he said nothing more.

'Is the garden all your work?' she asked him, unable to hide her surprise at the idea that *he* had been responsible for the expert landscaping.

He laughed. 'Hardly—it covers two acres, and I employ a team of gardeners to tend it. But in the beginning I did a lot of the spadework.' It had been strangely cathartic, digging the soil where once his family home had stood. He had come here day after day and worked until he was physically exhausted, but nothing had banished the dreams where he heard Cristina's voice begging him to save her and their unborn child.

He saw that Gina was staring at him. 'Why are you looking at me as if I've grown another head?'

'I don't get you,' she admitted frankly. 'I can't equate the daredevil playboy who loves dangerous sports like sky-diving with the man who counts gardening as one of his hobbies.'

He shrugged. 'But I don't need you to understand me, *cara*.'

Gina knew he had not meant to be deliberately hurtful, and that made it worse—because his careless comment was deeply wounding. She had known from the start that he only wanted an affair with her. Just because sometimes in the aftermath of their lovemaking she felt closer to him than she had to any other human being it did not mean that he felt the same way.

Lanzo never revealed his emotions. But presumably he must have been in love once, and that was why the portrait of his fiancée was displayed in the hallway of his house—so that her face was the first thing he saw every time he walked through the door.

Gina had sat down on the wall near to Lanzo, but now she jerked to her feet, wishing she had the nerve to ask him about his past. But why would he confide in her when he regarded her as just another temporary mistress? she thought bitterly. And why did she care? It wasn't as if he meant anything to her. In a few months his usual PA would return to work for him, and once Luisa was back Gina would leave him and get on with her life.

Oh, *hell*. Why did that thought hurt so much? And why was her head spinning again? Or was it the ground beneath her feet that was moving, tilting so that she was falling into blackness?

'Gina!'

Lanzo's voice came from far away. And then there was nothing.

'I do not need to see a doctor. I can't believe you've called the poor man out when it's obvious I must have fainted because I haven't eaten for hours.'

Gina glared at Lanzo, infuriated when he gave her a bland smile and pushed her gently back down so that she was lying on the sofa.

'I'm surprised you didn't break your back, carrying me to the house,' she muttered. 'I'm no lightweight.'

'Stop talking and lie quietly,' he advised her, a nuance in his tone warning her that she was wasting her breath arguing with him. 'You've been feeling unwell for a week, and it's sensible to have a check-up. The doctor is here now,' he said, getting to his feet at the sound of Daphne's voice, followed by a deeper tone, coming from the hall.

To Gina's annoyance Lanzo did not leave the room while the doctor took her blood pressure.

'That all seems fine,' the elderly doctor assured her. 'You say you have never fainted before?'

'Never—' Gina said firmly.

'But Signorina Bailey has felt dizzy on several occasions during the past week or so,' Lanzo interrupted.

'There could be a number of causes,' the doctor mused, 'one of which is pregnancy. Is there a possibility—?'

'No.' Gina cut him off. 'No possibility at all.' The words of the gynaecologist she had seen when she had still been married to Simon echoed in her head.

'I'm afraid the scarring caused by the endometriosis means that your only real hope of having a child is with IVF.'

'It's out of the question,' she insisted, when Dottore Casatelli gave her a searching glance.

'Well, there are many other reasons for feeling faint—anaemia is certainly a possibility. I suggest you come to my surgery so that I can perform a simple blood test.'

Gina nodded, her mind only half concentrating on what the doctor was saying as she did some mental arithmetic. Her period was late—over a week late—and she was amazed she hadn't noticed. When she had been trying for a baby with Simon she had plotted the exact date, almost the exact hour, her period should start, and being even a day late had sent her rushing to buy a pregnancy test kit—only to have her hopes dashed every time. Undoubtedly this was just a blip in her cycle.

She glanced distractedly at Lanzo when he excused himself to answer a phone call. After he had left the room she smiled politely at the doctor as he stood and picked up his medical bag, but her smile turned to a look of puzzlement when he handed her a small package.

'I don't need to do a pregnancy test,' she insisted. 'I suffer from a medical condition that makes it virtually impossible for me to conceive.'

'And yet sometimes the impossible is possible after all,' the doctor said gently. 'Do the test, *signorina*, if only so that we can eliminate pregnancy as a reason for your dizzy spells.'

It was a complete waste of time, Gina thought to herself half an hour later, as she sat on the edge of the marble bath and waited for the required two minutes to tick past. Fortunately Lanzo was holding a conference call with his office in Japan, and she had slipped upstairs to carry out the pregnancy test without his knowledge.

It was stupid to feel nervous. It was habit, she supposed.

In the past she had carried out dozens of tests, and had paced the bathroom feeling sick with a mixture of excitement and desperate hope that she would receive the result she was praying for. Of course this time she hoped the result would be negative—or rather not hoped, but simply assumed that she could not be pregnant. She checked her watch and leaned forward to look at the test—and felt her heart slam against her ribs.

Pregnant 5+. Only she wasn't. The test was wrong.

Thankfully the kit contained a second test, but her hands were shaking so much that she fumbled to rip off the packaging and carry out the instructions. A sense of numbness settled over Gina as she watched the hand on her watch crawl round. This time the result would be negative, and that would be for the best—because she wasn't in a position to have a baby right now. As for Lanzo… Well, she dared not contemplate what his reaction would be—but it was ridiculous to worry because she *wasn't* pregnant. The gynaecologist had been very gentle when she had explained that both her fallopian tubes were blocked.

The two minutes were up. Taking a deep breath, she checked the test—and disbelief slowly turned to incandescent joy as she stared at the word 'pregnant' in the result box.

Lanzo had gone out on his motorbike, Daphne informed Gina after she had plucked up the courage to go downstairs and face him. Her sense of relief that she had been given a brief reprieve before she broke her astounding news soon turned to dread at the thought of him hurtling at breakneck speed along the narrow road that corkscrewed along the coast. What if he had an accident and was thrown over the cliff-edge onto the jagged rocks below?

Stop it, she ordered herself firmly. Lanzo knew what he was doing. But he had told her that he did not fear death.

She stared out of the window at the sea sparkling in the summer sunshine and felt a shiver run through her at the idea of Lanzo being injured—or worse. She would have to bring up her child alone. But perhaps she would be doing that anyway, her brain pointed out. She might be overjoyed about this baby, but there was a possibility that Lanzo would not feel the same way.

By the time she heard the throb of the motorbike engine almost an hour later her nerves were as taut as an overstrung bow. Wiping her damp palms down her jeans, she hurried out to the hall just as he walked through the front door, and despite her tension she did not miss the way his eyes went immediately to the portrait of his dead fiancée. Neither did she miss the fact that he looked lethally sexy in his black biker leathers, and she closed her eyes briefly, wishing he did not make her feel like an over-awed eighteen-year-old.

Lanzo studied Gina's pale face and frowned. 'Are you feeling dizzy again?' he demanded, concern sweeping through him. He was puzzled too, wondering why she seemed distinctly on edge, and he noted that she was carefully avoiding his gaze. 'What's wrong, *cara*?'

'I need to talk to you.' She swallowed and glanced at the painting of his fiancée. 'But not here.'

'Come into my study.'

Gina would have preferred the lounge; his study was too formal, somehow, to discuss something as personal as the fact that she had conceived his child. When he closed the door she felt a crazy impulse to wrench it open again and run away.

He rounded his desk and sat down, indicating that she should do the same. But she remained standing, and it struck her as she darted him a nervous glance how forbidding he seemed, with his hard jaw and slashing cheekbones, and those curious green eyes that at this moment were coolly assessing her.

'What is the matter, Gina?' he asked again.

Her heart was thumping, and she was sure it could not be good for the baby. Dear heaven, she thought shakily, the baby—she was going to have a *baby*. It still seemed unreal.

She took a deep breath and met his gaze. 'I'm…pregnant. The doctor gave me a pregnancy test—he said it would be a good idea to rule out the possibility,' she continued quickly, when Lanzo made no response. For once he wasn't wearing sunglasses, but she still had no idea what he was thinking. She wished he would say something; his silence was shredding her nerves. 'It…the test…was positive.'

Everything inside Lanzo rejected Gina's shocking statement. For a few seconds his brain simply would not accept it could be true, but common sense told him there was no reason why she would have made it up. His next thought was to acknowledge that he did not want it to be true. But it seemed that fate could not give a damn about what he wanted, he thought savagely.

She was watching him, and seemed to be waiting for him to say something. What was he supposed to say? *Congratulations?* he wondered sardonically. *How wonderful? Dio*, he felt as though his life had ended—and in a way it had, he realised grimly. Because, whatever happened now, his life was never going to be quite the same. If Gina was really expecting his child, he would be responsible for her and the baby.

He felt trapped by the situation that had been thrust upon him, and a feeling of mingled dread and panic filled him. Fifteen years ago he had failed to protect his fiancée and his unborn child. He knew he could not have prevented the fire, but if he had stayed at home with Cristina, as she had begged him to do, he could have saved all of them. He would have married the woman he had loved, his parents would have seen their grandchild, and his child would now be a teenager.

The familiar feeling of guilt that he had not been there for Cristina surged through him. The pain of losing her had almost destroyed him, and he had vowed that he would never allow himself to care for anyone else. He did not allow himself to feel emotions, and he was certain he would feel nothing for the child Gina had told him she was carrying.

'How could it happen?' he asked harshly. There had only been that first night when they had become lovers when he had not used protection, but she had assured him it was safe. 'You told me you were on the pill.'

'I...' Gina frowned, startled by his assertion. 'I didn't say that.'

'You said there was no risk,' he drawled, in a dangerously soft tone.

She had expected him to be angry, Gina acknowledged. He had a typical Latin temperament, and she had steeled herself for a blast of his explosive temper. Nothing had prepared her for this cold, controlled fury.

'I didn't mean that I was on the pill....' Gina bit her lip. 'When I told you there was no risk that I could fall pregnant I was absolutely certain that was true,' she said urgently. 'I believed I was infertile. I...I tried for over a year to have a baby with Simon, and when nothing happened I had various tests which revealed that I have a condition called endometriosis. It's a common cause of infertility, and further tests showed that my fallopian tubes were so badly scarred that my only hope of having a child was with medical intervention such as IVF.'

She pushed her hair back from her face with a shaky hand and stared at Lanzo, silently pleading for him to understand. 'This baby…' She swallowed the tears that clogged her throat. 'The fact that I am pregnant is nothing short of a miracle, and although I accept that the circumstances are not ideal, I have to be honest and tell you that I am overjoyed that my dream of having a baby might come true.'

He stared back at her, his face hard and implacable, his eyes still coldly accusing. 'It might be *your* dream,' he said harshly, 'but it is not mine. I do not want a child, and I have always taken scrupulous care to ensure that I would not father one. The fact that you have accidentally fallen pregnant does not alter how I feel.'

A child needed to be loved, but he had no love inside him, Lanzo brooded. All his emotions had withered and died the night of the fire, and it would be better for the child Gina carried to grow up without him instead of yearning for the father's love that he simply could not give.

Gina shivered, reaction setting in both to the astounding news that she was expecting Lanzo's baby and his insistence that he did not want a child. She did not know what she had expected from him. It was only natural that he was shocked by her news, but she had assumed that once he had grown used to the idea they would discuss how they would bring the baby up—together.

A wave of fierce maternal protectiveness surged through Gina. *She* wanted the fragile life nestled inside her, and she would love and care for her child on her own. Lanzo need not be involved in any way. But it was only fair to make clear to him that—fate willing—she *was* going to have this baby.

'I'm sorry you feel that way,' she said quietly. 'But the fact is that because of the endometriosis this is probably my only chance to be a mother, and nothing could persuade me to terminate my pregnancy.'

Lanzo jerked his head back as if she had slapped him. '*Dio*, I do not expect that,' he said, as shocked as he had been minutes earlier, when she had told him she was pregnant.

The idea was repugnant to him. But did that mean then that he *wanted* her to have his child? He could not think straight. His brain was reeling. He stood up abruptly, the sound of his chair legs scraping on the tiled floor shattering the tense silence.

'I accept that I am partly responsible for the problem,' he said tersely. 'When I come back we will discuss a financial settlement for the child.'

His stark words caused something inside Gina to shatter. 'Come back from where?' she asked shakily.

'I'm going out on the bike.' He had already snatched up his crash helmet, and did not look at her as he strode towards the door.

Fear that he would ride too fast turned to a slow-burning anger that he was prepared to walk away from his child.

'That's right—go and endanger your life for the sheer hell of it,' she said bitterly. 'That just about sums you up, Lanzo—you'd do anything to avoid a discussion that might in any way involve your emotions.'

He stopped dead and jerked his head round, his face so dark with fury that she took an involuntary step backwards. But as the silence stretched between them the expression in his eyes changed and became bleak, almost haunted. Without another word he strode out of the room, slamming the door behind him with such force that the sound echoed in her head long after he had gone.

CHAPTER EIGHT

RICHARD MELTON and his wife, Sarah—Gina's stepsister—lived in a recently built house on the outskirts of Poole. Lanzo parked in the narrow cul-de-sac and glanced at the six identical houses built in a semi-circle. The Meltons lived at number four. As he walked up the path to the front door he could see a baby's crib in the front living room, and he felt his heart give a curious little lurch, even though he knew that it was not *his* child sleeping within the wicker basket.

The Meltons' baby was two months old: a boy, so Gina had informed him during their one short telephone conversation, when he had struggled to hear her over the high-pitched wailing of a newborn infant. That had been pretty well all that she had said—apart from explaining that she had not answered his calls to her mobile because she did not want to speak to him.

There had been little point in him tracking down her whereabouts through her brother-in-law, she had told him coldly. For, desperate to find her, Lanzo had recalled that Richard Melton ran a company called Nautica World, and he had eventually persuaded the other man to give him a phone number where he could contact Gina, on the strict understanding that he did not upset her.

They had nothing to say to one another, she had continued, her voice stiff with pride. She was well, and there were no problems with her pregnancy—an early scan had shown that she was eight weeks pregnant—and she was managing just fine, thank you. She would appreciate it if he did not phone again.

What did she expect him to do? Twiddle his thumbs for the next seven months and hope she remembered to send him a 'baby's arrived' card? That was probably what she *did* expect him to do, he thought heavily as he pressed the front doorbell. Certainly he had not expected her to have left his home in Positano when he'd returned from racing his motorbike along the winding road that hugged the Amalfi Coast. He had only been gone for an hour, needing time to come to terms with her announcement that she was expecting his baby. His shock had receded now, but his fundamental feeling had not changed. He still did not want to be a father.

A harassed-looking woman clutching a toddler in her arms opened the front door.

'Yes, Gina's in,' Sarah Melton admitted begrudgingly, eyeing him with deep suspicion when he introduced himself. 'But I'm not sure she'll want to see you.'

'Why don't we allow Gina to decide for herself?' Lanzo said, polite but determined, edging his foot over the doorstep as he spoke. He frowned as the unmistakable sound of somebody being sick came from upstairs.

'She's in the loo—throwing up. It's a pretty regular occurrence,' Sarah said wryly. 'You'd better come in and wait.'

Gina wiped her face with a damp flannel, her whole body trembling from the effort of losing her lunch twenty minutes after she had eaten it. The same thing had happened after breakfast. At this rate she might as well cut out the middle man and simply flush her meals down the toilet, she thought dismally.

'Unfortunately a small percentage of women suffer from extreme morning sickness,' her GP had explained. 'And, as you are no doubt aware, it is not only limited to mornings. Your baby will be perfectly all right,' he'd reassured her, when she had been close to tears, terrified that she might miscarry the baby. 'All I can recommend is plenty of fluids, small meals, and plenty of rest.'

Out of the three, she was just about managing the fluids. Food of any type bounced back with tedious regularity, and as for resting—it was proving impossible to sleep when she was so worried about how she was going to manage as a single mother, and if she did manage to drop off in the early hours her dreams were haunted by Lanzo.

She opened the bathroom door and staggered along the landing to the tiny boxroom where Sarah and Richard had put up a camp bed for her, after she had fled from Lanzo's home in Italy and arrived back in Poole, homeless and distraught.

Golden late-September sunshine was streaming through the window, so that the tall figure standing by the bed was silhouetted against the light. But the broad shoulders and the proud tilt of his head were instantly recognizable, and she stopped dead in the doorway, acute shock causing her heart to beat so fast that she could feel it jerking against her ribs.

'What are you doing here?' she demanded, cursing herself for the distinct wobble in her voice.

'We need to talk,' Lanzo said steadily.

His deep, sensual accent tugged on her heartstrings, and she hated the fact that the sight of him, after three weeks apart, made her knees feel weak. It did not help that he looked utterly gorgeous, in black jeans and matching polo shirt, topped with a butter-soft tan leather jacket. His hair was shorter than she remembered, gleaming like raw silk in the sunlight, and his face was all angles and planes, softened by the beautifully shaped mouth that she had a vivid recall of moving hungrily over her lips when he kissed her.

From his shocked expression it was clear that kissing her was not on his agenda now, she thought grimly. She caught sight of her reflection in the mirror and saw what he could see—grey skin, dull eyes with great purple smudges beneath them, and lank hair scraped back in a ponytail.

'You look terrible,' he said bluntly, as if he could not hold back the words.

Despite telling herself she didn't care what he thought of her, tears stung her eyes. 'I doubt you would look so great if you were sick a dozen times a day,' she muttered.

Lanzo frowned. 'I know sickness is common in early pregnancy, but is it normal to be sick so frequently?'

'Do you care?' Pride was her only shield against the note of concern in his voice. He had made it clear that he did not care about her or the baby, she reminded herself.

He sighed heavily. '*Si*, I care about your well-being, Gina. That is why I am here—to make sure that you have everything you need.' He glanced around the cramped room, at the uncomfortable-looking camp bed and at her clothes piled on a chair and spilling out of her suitcase because there was no space to put a wardrobe.

'Your brother-in-law told me you are living here.'

'Temporarily,' Gina said shortly. 'If you remember, I rented out my flat when I started working for you, and the tenancy agreement runs until December.'

'So, do you then plan to move back into your flat? I thought there was a mortgage on it. How do you intend to meet the monthly payments when the baby is born and you cannot work?' Lanzo pushed for answers to the questions that had been circling endlessly in Gina's mind since her mad dash back to England. She avoided his gaze and sank weakly down onto the camp bed, which creaked alarmingly.

'I'm going to sell the flat and buy somewhere...' She had been about to say *cheaper*, but she refused to reveal her money worries to Lanzo and so mumbled, 'Somewhere more suitable to bring up the baby.'

He stared speculatively at her pale face and his stomach clenched. She looked so fragile, so unlike the strong-willed, confident Gina he was used to. His eyes dropped to her flat stomach. If anything she looked thinner than he remembered—perhaps not surprising, if she was being sick numerous times a day. He wondered if she was eating properly, getting the necessary vitamins and nutrients for the baby to develop. It was hard to believe that his child was growing within her when there were no outward signs of her pregnancy, he mused. Yet he sensed a difference in her—a vulnerability that filled him with guilt.

'Are you working?' he asked abruptly, thinking that her obvious tiredness might be because she was overdoing things.

Gina twisted her fingers together, tension churning inside her. 'Not at the moment,' she admitted. 'It's been impossible to look for a job when I'm constantly being sick. But hopefully I'll feel better in another week or so, and then...' She tailed off, trying to imagine how she would cope with holding down a full-time job when she had no energy and felt like a limp rag.

'So how are you managing financially?'

'I have some savings.' That were dwindling fast—but she was not going to tell Lanzo that. 'Look,' she said, jumping to her feet and immediately wishing she hadn't when the room swayed, 'I don't know why you're here…'

Her legs were so stupidly wobbly. She felt her knees give way, but before she fell Lanzo was beside her, sliding his arm around her waist to support her. The scent of his aftershave assailed her senses and she felt a crazy longing to rest her cheek against his broad chest and absorb some of his strength.

'I am here because it is my responsibility to help you,' he murmured.

She rejected his words violently, jerking away from him. 'No. I am *not* your responsibility, and neither is my baby. You made it clear that you don't want your child.'

Lanzo glimpsed the hurt in her eyes and sighed heavily. 'Sit down, *cara*, before you fall down.' He helped her back down onto the camp bed and hunkered down next to her. 'I did some research about the condition you suffer from, and I accept that you were convinced you were infertile because of the damage done by endometriosis,' he said quietly.

'I was about to start a course of IVF when I was with Simon, but our marriage was struggling as his drink problem grew worse and I knew it wouldn't be fair to bring a child into that situation,' she explained huskily. 'I believed I would never have a baby. But now I have this one chance, I'm terrified something is going to go wrong,' she whispered, her deepest fears spilling out. 'I know you don't want a child, but I don't think I could bear it if I lost this baby.'

Once again her vulnerability evoked an ache inside Lanzo, but he knew his limitations—knew he could not give her the emotional support she needed—and so he resisted the urge to take her in his arms and hold her close while he soothed her fears.

'I am not capable of being a father,' he told her harshly.

Startled blue eyes flew to his face. 'What do you mean? There's no question that this is your baby. You're the only man I've slept with since Simon—and that side of our marriage ended long before the divorce,' she added heavily.

'I'm not denying that you are carrying my child.' A corner of Lanzo's mind registered that he had been her only lover after she had ended her relationship with her abusive husband, and he wondered why the knowledge made him so inordinately pleased.

'I cannot love a child. I cannot love anyone—it is simply not part of my psyche,' he insisted, irritated by the flash of sympathy in her eyes. 'It's not a problem, *cara*. I like the fact that my life is free from the emotional debris that most people have to deal with. But I realise that a child needs to feel loved, and I'm sure you would agree that it would not be fair on this baby to grow up yearning for something I cannot give it.'

'But…' Gina stared at him, utterly nonplussed by his shocking confession. She had thought that he exerted iron control over his emotions, but according to Lanzo he did not *have* the normal range of emotions most people had, and it was impossible for him to love anyone—even his own child. 'Daphne told me that you were once engaged—to the girl whose portrait hangs in the hallway of the Villa di Sussurri. Didn't—didn't you love *her*?' she faltered.

His hard face was expressionless, but she sensed the sudden tension that gripped him. 'That was a long time ago. I was a different person then to the man I am now,' he said harshly.

Lanzo rose to his feet and took the two steps needed to cross the small room to the window, which overlooked the neat front lawn and the five other neat front lawns of the other houses in the cul-de-sac.

'Although I cannot be a proper father, I have a duty to

provide financial security for our child, and for you. Yes,'
he said firmly when Gina opened her mouth to argue. 'It
is the one thing I can give—the one part I can play in our
child's life. And you need my help.' He glanced at her, so
pale and strained, sitting on the precarious camp bed. From
downstairs came the sound of a baby crying, mingled with
the yells of two small children, and Gina's stepsister's raised
voice.

'It cannot be ideal living here—for you or your family.
I want you to live at my house on Sandbanks. You won't
be able to sleep on this contraption in a few months, when
your pregnancy is more advanced,' he pointed out, glancing again at the camp bed. 'There are five bedrooms at
Ocean View House, and a big garden for when the baby is
walking.'

'Walking! That won't be for a couple of years from now.'
Gina had a sudden image of a toddler taking his or her first
steps, and she felt a mixture of joyful anticipation and fear
for the future.

She still couldn't quite believe she was pregnant. Her GP,
who was aware of her medical history, had agreed it was
nothing short of a miracle that she had conceived naturally,
and she was acutely conscious that this could be her only
chance to have a baby. *Please let me carry the baby full-
term and let it be born safely,* she prayed silently.

But right now there were other problems to be dealt
with. She looked at Lanzo. 'I can't stay at your house all
that time.'

'It will be your house,' he told her. 'Yours and the
baby's—I have already instructed my lawyer to arrange for
the deeds to be transferred to your name. And naturally I
will cover all your living costs.'

'I don't want your money,' she said sharply.

'Cara...' He admired her stubborn pride, but she had

to accept that she needed him. 'Let me help you—for our child's sake. I've explained why I feel it is better if I am not involved in its upbringing, but I want you and the baby to live comfortably. You can't say you are doing that here— however welcoming your stepsister and her husband might be,' he said gently.

He had cleverly brought up the subject that was on her mind constantly, for there was no doubt that although she and Sarah had always got on well it was awkward staying here, and Gina felt that she was imposing on her stepsister's goodwill. It wasn't even as if she was much help with the new baby and her other two nephews when she spent so much time being sick, she acknowledged ruefully.

But how could she live in Lanzo's house and allow him to support her financially? It went against everything she believed in. She was proud of the fact that she had always worked since she had left school, and always paid her own way. She could not work at the moment, though. No employer would take her on when she had to rush to the toilet every half an hour.

'It would be a great help if I could live at Ocean View at least until after the baby is born,' she said quietly. 'But as soon as the morning sickness has passed I will look for a job.'

Lanzo frowned. 'There is no need for you to work.'

'Yes, there is. I don't really understand why you feel that you can't be a proper father to the baby,' she admitted, 'but I will love him or her enough for both of us. If you wish to support our child financially that's up to you, but I have never cared about your money, Lanzo.'

She pushed away the thought that she cared too much about *him*. If he could not love his own child he was hardly likely to fall in love with her. There wasn't much point in denying that she had secretly hoped he would, she thought bleakly. For whatever reason—and she suspected it had a lot to do with losing his fiancée—Lanzo believed that he was incapable of loving anyone, and she would just have to accept that fact.

To Gina's surprise, everything proved to be so much easier than she had expected. Lanzo helped her pack her clothes, and took her to his house on Sandbanks the same day he had turned up out of the blue at her stepsister's house. She did not know what he'd said to Sarah and Richard, but when she walked downstairs, clutching a carrier bag stuffed with hastily packed toiletries, they were chatting to him as if he were a long-lost brother—and she detected Sarah's relief that she was moving into his house, thereby freeing up the spare room.

'Daphne is going to stay here to cook and run the house,' Lanzo explained when the housekeeper greeted them at the front door of Ocean View, and led them into the lounge where she served a gorgeous tea of scones, jam and rich clotted cream.

'Maybe three scones was pushing my luck,' Gina said ruefully, emerging from the bathroom a short while later, after losing most of the meal.

Lanzo looked grimly at her wan face. 'You can't carry on like this. It's not good for you or the baby.'

'My GP assures me that the baby won't be affected, however many times a day I'm sick. It will take all the nutrients it needs from the small amount of food I manage to keep down. As long as the baby is okay, I don't care about me,' she said cheerfully, unaware that she resembled a fragile ghost to Lanzo's concerned eyes.

'Daphne will prepare you lots of small meals, and she is under orders to make sure you get plenty of rest,' he told her, the following morning as he was about to leave for a business trip. 'I'm going to New York to check on the progress of building work after the fire, and from there down to Florida, before I fly to Moscow. But I'll keep in contact.'

It was on the tip of her tongue to assure him that it was not necessary for him to phone her. She accepted that he did not want to have a role in their baby's life, and there was no reason for him to call her. But part of her—the silly, emotional part, she thought derisively—was glad that he intended to keep in touch…even if it was only through the occasional phone call. So she changed the subject and asked curiously, 'Are you planning to open a Di Cosimo restaurant in Florida?'

He slung his case onto the back seat of his car and glanced at her standing on the front steps of the house. 'No, I'm competing in a powerboat race in Miami.'

Gina bit her lip. Only recently the son of a well-known English multimillionaire had been killed when his powerboat had flipped over during a race. The story had been headline news, and she had felt sick when she had read it. It was stupid to wish that Lanzo would stay here with her, at his beautiful house overlooking the harbour, and wait for their baby to be born. He would probably die of boredom, she thought sadly. He was addicted to dangerous sports and he was not interested in the baby.

She bit back the words *be careful*, and said coolly, 'Have fun.'

Lanzo nodded and slid behind the wheel of the car, wondering why he felt a sudden urge to send one of his staff to New York. Gina would be perfectly all right with Daphne to take care of her, he reminded himself. Ocean View, like all his houses, had the most up-to-date fire alarm and sprinkler system fitted. Nothing could happen to her. But she looked so forlorn as she waved to him, and he was reminded suddenly of the day ten years ago, when he had dropped her back to her father's farm and told her that he was returning to Italy.

He recalled the shock in her eyes, the shimmer of tears that she had blinked fiercely to dispel, and remembered feeling the same hollow ache inside that he felt now. Of course he had known she was in love with him. It was one reason why he had decided to leave Poole, for he had not wanted to hurt her. It was only when he had brushed his mouth over hers in one last kiss and felt her tremble with emotion that he had realised he had probably broken her heart. But she was young—only eighteen and just starting out on life's journey—he had told himself as he had driven away. She would soon get over him.

And clearly she had—and had gone on to have a good career, get married... His jaw hardened when he thought of the scar on her neck caused by her alcoholic ex-husband. Gina was a beautiful person, inside and out, and she deserved a far better life than she had had with Simon. But instead she had conceived *his* child, and he had bluntly told her that he could not give her any emotional support. He had given her a house and an allowance, to appease his conscience, and was about to drive off and leave her to cope with her pregnancy alone.

What else could he do? he thought savagely as he swung out of the front gates and glanced back at her in his rearview mirror. There was an empty void inside him where his heart had once been, and it would be better for all of them if he remained a remote figure in Gina and the baby's lives. Maybe she would meet someone else in the future—some guy who would love her as she deserved to be loved. After all, he could not expect her to live the life of a nun, he reasoned.

The thought turned his mood to one of simmering black

fury, and when he reached the motorway he pressed his foot down on the accelerator pedal and shot into the fast lane.

Gina watched Lanzo's car turn out of the drive and then slowly walked back into the house, fighting the stupid urge to burst into tears. After his furious reaction when she had told him she was pregnant, she had left his villa in Positano within the hour and assumed that she would never see or hear from him again. She was still reeling from the shock of him turning up in Poole yesterday. Once again he had hurtled into her life like a tornado, and before she could blink she had found herself agreeing to live at his house on Sandbanks.

She could not deny that it was a relief not to have to worry about where she and the baby would live, but seeing Lanzo again had forced her to acknowledge that she had committed the ultimate folly and fallen in love with him. They had been friends as well as lovers, and the weeks she had worked for him and travelled the world with him had been the happiest time of her life, she thought softly, her heart aching as memories of laughter, long conversations, and nights of heady passion assailed her.

Now he had gone again, and part of her wished he had never sought her out—because for a few hope-filled moments she had assumed that he had come because he wanted her and the baby, and the realisation that the only part he intended to play in her life was that of benefactor had shattered her dreams.

She wandered aimlessly into the lounge and watched a fishing boat chug out of the harbour. A few minutes later Daphne came in, carrying a tray.

'I've brought you a snack. Hopefully you'll keep it down,' the housekeeper said with a sympathetic smile.

'Thank you.' Gina hesitated. 'Daphne, what happened to Lanzo's fiancée—I mean…how did she die?'

Daphne lively face instantly became shuttered. 'There was a terrible accident. Cristina and Lanzo's parents were all killed.' She hurried over to the door. 'Excuse me—I've left something in the oven,' she muttered, and disappeared before Gina could question her further.

Why was Daphne so reluctant to talk about what had happened? she wondered frustratedly. And why did Lanzo never mention his past? It must have been devastating to lose the woman he planned to marry and his parents, in one terrible event. She was sure that the accident was the key to understanding why he had locked his emotions away, but the only two people who knew what had happened refused to speak.

Lanzo phoned from New York and told her that the fire-damaged restaurant had been refitted and would open the following week. He phoned again from Miami, to say that he had won the powerboat race, and a few days later he called from Moscow, where he was planning to open another Di Cosimo restaurant.

As the weeks slipped by he settled into a pattern of phoning two or three times a week, and Gina looked forward to his calls. Lucky him, to be in the hot sunshine of the Caribbean when October storms were lashing the English south coast, she told him. And did he really expect her to be sympathetic because he was melting in the forty-degree heat in Perth, when she had woken up to find a white blanket of frost covering the lawn at Ocean View?

His husky laugh evoked a warm feeling inside her that banished the gloom of the cold November day. Somehow it was easier to talk to him when he was thousands of miles away. Released from her intense physical awareness of him, she was able to relax and chat to him with the easy friendship that they had shared when she had been his PA.

Her morning sickness gradually subsided, and as her energy levels shot up she was glad to find a part-time job as secretary to a local councillor.

'I'm not overdoing it,' she told Lanzo, when he sounded distinctly unenthusiastic about her new job. 'The most strenuous activity I do is walk across the office to the filing cabinet.'

'There's no need for you to work,' Lanzo growled as he stared out of his hotel window in Bangkok. He was tempted to catch the next available flight to England, to check that Gina really was as fit and well as she assured him. 'Why don't you use the money I've put into the bank account I opened for you?'

'I prefer to pay my own way,' she said crisply. She was determined not to touch his money, and it was lucky that she was earning again—because time had flown past and she was now nearly five months pregnant, with a sizeable bump. She loved wandering around the mother-and-baby shops, choosing maternity clothes as well as tiny newborn-sized vests and sleepsuits that she put away in the room she had decided would be the nursery.

She could not believe her pregnancy was passing so quickly, she mused, when she woke up on Christmas Day and ticked off another week on her calendar. Her due date was at the end of April, and she was finally daring to believe that the miracle *would* happen and she would soon be holding her baby in her arms.

She half expected Lanzo to call on Christmas morning, and delayed leaving for lunch with her family, hating herself for hovering near the phone. He had told her he was spending the festive period in Rome, mainly because his new PA—who was filling in until Luisa returned from maternity leave—lived in the city. He was snowed under with work at the moment, and Raphaella had agreed to come over to his apartment to help him catch up on paperwork.

She bit her lip. Maybe Raphaella, who had sounded incredibly sexy when she had answered Lanzo's mobile phone once, when Gina had called to tell him that her second scan had been fine, was helping him with more than his paperwork? He had a high sex-drive, and it was impossible to believe he had spent the past few months celibate.

The idea of him making love to another woman made her stomach churn, and she pulled on her coat and wrenched open the front door, desperate to be with people who cared for her, rather than alone with her jealous thoughts.

'Happy Christmas, *cara*.'

'L…Lanzo?' The disbelief in her voice caused his lips to curve into a lazy smile.

'Well, I'm definitely not Babbo Natale.'

'I guessed that by the lack of red suit and long white beard,' she said huskily, her heart thudding as her eyes roamed over his pale jeans and the chunky oatmeal-coloured sweater beneath his suede jacket. 'What are you doing here? I mean…' She flushed, remembering how she had imagined him getting close and personal with the sexy-sounding Raphaella. 'I thought you were in Rome.'

Lanzo had thought of half a dozen excuses for why he needed to come to England, but as he stared at Gina, struck by how beautiful she looked in a wine-coloured soft woollen dress that clung to the rounded contours of her breasts and the swollen mound of her stomach, he could not deny the truth.

'I wanted to spend Christmas with you,' he said simply.

Shock rendered Gina speechless, but a little bubble of happiness formed inside her, and grew and grew until it seemed to encompass every inch of her. She wanted to throw herself into his arms and kiss him, until he kissed her back and then carried her into the house and upstairs to bed. But the thought that he would struggle to carry her more than a few feet now that she had gained weight, combined with the fear that he would not find her pregnant shape attractive, stopped her. Instead she smiled, and her heart lurched when he smiled back, his green eyes gleaming as he walked up the front steps.

Reality caught up with her. 'I'm supposed to be having lunch with Dad and Linda. There's not much to eat here, because Daphne has gone to visit her sister for Christmas and I told her not to stock up the larder as I would be with my family.'

Lanzo shrugged. 'I don't expect you to change your arrangements for me. Go to your family, and I'll see you later.'

Gina shook her head. 'You can't spend Christmas Day alone.' She hesitated. 'You could come with me, if you like. I know my stepmother won't mind—she always cooks enough to feed an army anyway. Sarah and Hazel and their families will be there.' She gave him a rueful smile. 'It will be hectic, but fun. But if you'd rather not…'

It had been more than fifteen years since Lanzo had enjoyed Christmas with his parents and Cristina. He was glad he had not known at the time that it would be the last Christmas he would ever spend with them.

He pushed the memories to the back of his mind and smiled at Gina. 'I'd love to come,' he said softly. 'Does your father drink wine? I've got six bottles of a rather excellent burgundy in the boot of my car.'

CHAPTER NINE

GINA had fallen asleep on the sofa. It was hardly surprising after an enormous lunch and a noisy afternoon playing with her nephews and nieces, Lanzo mused. Christmas with her family had been as hectic as she had warned, but after an initial few minutes of awkwardness on all sides he had been surprised by how warmly he had been received by her father, stepmother, and stepsisters.

He stretched out his long legs and watched the twinkling fairy lights on the tree Gina had put up in the lounge at Ocean View. He never bothered with tinsel and baubles and all the other tacky decorations that came with the festive season. Whether he spent Christmas at his villa in Positano or at his apartment in Rome, the day meant nothing to him. It was a time of celebration, of families coming together, but he had no family.

He thought again of how welcome he had been made to feel by Gina's family. This time next year the baby would be here, but he would not come to England to spend Christmas with his child. It wouldn't be fair when he could not be a proper, loving father—like Gina's stepsisters' husbands were to their children. When he had watched Richard Melton cradling his infant son he had felt guilty, because he knew he would not love his child. Since he had lost Cristina he had hardened his heart and shunned any relationship that might involve his emotions. Nothing touched him, or moved him, and he liked the fact that his life was uncomplicated, he reminded himself.

Gina stirred and turned her head towards Lanzo, but she remained asleep, her long lashes lying against her cheeks and her chest rising and falling steadily. She had always been delightfully curvaceous, but pregnancy had made her breasts fuller—big and rounded beneath her soft woollen dress. The temptation to touch them and feel their weight was so strong that he inhaled sharply, his nostrils flaring as desire corkscrewed through him.

He had been too long without sex, he though grimly. It was months since he had made love to Gina, but he had no inclination to take another mistress. It did not seem right to sleep with another woman when his child was growing inside Gina. Perhaps when the child was born he would find it easier to distance himself from her. But right now all he could think of was peeling her dress down and baring those big, firm breasts. He wondered if her nipples were bigger too, and he shifted his position to try and ease the discomfort of his rock hard erection as he imagined sucking on each dusky crest.

'Lanzo… I'm sorry, I must have dropped off for a few minutes.' Gina opened her eyes, blushing when she realised that she had slid down the sofa so that her head had practically been resting on Lanzo's shoulder. 'You must be bored stiff, sitting here in the dark,' she mumbled, glancing around the shadowed room that was lit only by the colourful lights on the Christmas tree and the flickering flames of the fire.

One area of his anatomy was certainly stiff, he acknowledged derisively. 'I'm not bored, *cara*.' She was like a small soft kitten, snuggled up against him, and his heart gave a curious jerk as he lifted his hand to smooth her hair back from her face. 'It's peaceful, sitting here with you.'

After she had left Positano he had focused on work to prevent himself from thinking about her or the child she carried. Fifteen-hour days and constant travel around the world for Di Cosimo Holdings had allowed him little time to think about anything but business. But despite his self-imposed punishing schedule she had always been on his mind, and their long conversations when he phoned her from one faceless hotel or another had become addictive.

His desire for her had not faded in the months they had been apart. Memories of her gorgeous body had plagued his dreams, and now pregnancy had made her even more voluptuous and desirable.

The tick-tock of the clock on the mantelpiece was the only sound to break the silence. In the dusky dark of the barely lit room Lanzo's eyes gleamed with sensual intent, and Gina caught her breath when he slowly lowered his head. She knew he was going to kiss her, and she knew she should not let him, but she could not move.

Her lips parted.

'Cara...' His breath whispered across her skin, and that first brush of his mouth over hers was so sweetly beguiling that tears burned her eyes.

She could not resist him. And that, she thought ruefully, was the problem. She had fallen in love with him when she was eighteen, and deep down she knew that she had never fallen out of love with him.

He had missed her, Lanzo acknowledged, sliding his hand to her nape and angling her head so that he could deepen the kiss. Her lips were soft and moist, opening obediently to the firm probing of his tongue so that he could taste her. Heat flared inside him, and he groaned as hunger clawed in his gut, his body shaking with need. He cupped her breast and stroked his finger over the hard peak of her nipple, jutting beneath her dress, smiling against her lips when he heard her gasp.

Her need was as great as his. She had never been able to hide her intensely passionate nature from him, and her eager response increased his impatience to slide his throbbing shaft between her soft thighs. He moved his hand down and traced the curve of her stomach—and stiffened with shock when he felt a fluttering sensation beneath his fingertips.

'The baby is saying hello,' Gina murmured, feeling another, stronger flutter deep inside her. The sensation of her baby kicking was indescribably beautiful, and she held her hand over Lanzo's so that he could feel it again. 'Maybe he or she recognises their daddy,' she whispered. Her smile faltered when she saw his tense face. 'It's okay. It's quite normal for the baby to kick,' she assured him, thinking that he was worried something was wrong.

Lanzo jerked away from her as if he had been burned. The unguarded hope in her eyes had brought him crashing back to reality, and he raked his hand impatiently through his hair, cursing himself for allowing the situation to get out of hand. He should not have kissed her. But he had never been able to resist her.

'I've told you—I can't be the kind of father you want me to be,' he said harshly. 'I saw you watching your brother-in-law with his baby today, and I knew what you were thinking. But I will feel nothing for the child you are carrying when it is born—just as I feel nothing for anyone.'

'How can you be so certain?' Gina cried. 'When the baby is here you might feel differently.'

'I won't.' He stood up and snapped on one of the table lamps, the bright light it emitted throwing his hard features into sharp relief. He saw the hurt in her eyes and guilt gnawed at him. But there was no point in giving her false hope. 'I don't *want* to care for anyone,' he admitted.

'But why?' Gina ignored the painful tug on her heart. She had never realistically expected him to fall in love with her, but her baby would need its father to nurture and protect it, and most important of all to love it. She caught hold of his arm and clung to him when he would have pulled away.

'I know the way you feel is linked with losing your fiancée and your parents,' she said urgently. 'Daphne told me there had been an accident, but she won't talk about it.' She stared at him, willing him to talk to her and explain *why* he was so sure he could not love their child. But his expression was shuttered, and after a tense few seconds she allowed her hand to fall helplessly to her side and stepped back from him.

'I have to go,' he said roughly.

With stunned eyes she watched him stride over to the door. His jacket was lying on the back of a chair, and when he slung it over his shoulder the realisation sunk in that he was actually leaving.

'Where are you going? It's Christmas Day.' A day that had begun with such joy and hope and was ending in bleak despair. 'Surely there won't be any transport?'

'My private jet is on standby. I'll make a brief stop-over in Rome, before flying to Canada.' Work, as ever, would fill the void inside him. Discussions to open a new restaurant in Toronto would keep his mind occupied for several days.

Gina stumbled after him into the hall. His holdall was still there, where he had dropped it before they had gone to lunch with her family. He picked it up and opened the front door, so that a blast of icy air blew in.

She could not believe he was going. Surely he would turn back to her? Say something? He stepped out into the porch, and as he began to pull the door shut behind him her muscles unlocked and she ran forward.

'*Lanzo!*' She let out a shaky breath when he slowly turned his head, but the dull, dead expression in his eyes tore at her heart. 'Our baby needs you,' she whispered. She swallowed her pride and stared at him pleadingly. '*I* need you.'

He shook his head, as if to dismiss her words. 'I'm sorry, *cara*,' he said quietly, and strode down the steps to his car without looking back.

January brought snow to Dorset. Gina opened the curtains one morning to find that the garden had been transformed into a winter wonderland, and the sight of a red-breasted robin hopping over the white lawn brought a faint smile to her lips for the first time in weeks.

She told Lanzo about the snow when he phoned that evening. It was only the third time he had called since his abrupt departure on Christmas Day, and apart from his warning her not to drive the car if the roads were at all icy their conversation was stilted and painfully polite. She ended the call with the excuse that Daphne was about to serve dinner.

It was frightening how distant he had become, she thought dismally. The easy friendship they had once shared had disappeared, and it seemed as though they were strangers rather than two people who would become parents in a few short months. But Lanzo had been adamant that he would not be a father to their child. His only input would be to send regular cheques—presumably to appease his conscience, she thought bitterly.

The snow did not last for more than a few days before it turned to slush, and winter continued as grey and miserable as Gina's mood. And then one morning she woke to find that the bed was wet. Puzzled, she threw back the sheet—and for a moment her heart stopped beating, before she screamed for Daphne to come quickly.

'Explain to me exactly what placenta previa means?' Lanzo demanded, his jaw rigid with tension as spoke to the doctor in the hospital corridor outside the ward where Gina had been brought by ambulance earlier in the day.

'You are Miss Bailey's partner, I understand?' the doctor said, glancing down at his notes.

'*Si.*' Lanzo could not hide him impatience. 'I am the father of her child.' A father who had been hundreds of miles away in Rome when he had received Daphne's urgent phone call to tell him that Gina had been rushed into hospital because she was bleeding heavily, he thought grimly. He swallowed, and found that for some reason it hurt his throat to do so. 'There is no danger that Gina could lose the baby?'

'Fortunately the bleeding has stopped. But an ultrasound scan has revealed that your partner's placenta is lying partially across the cervix, which means that Miss Bailey will be unable to give birth naturally because of the risk of her haemorrhaging. She will need to have a Caesarean section,' the doctor continued. 'If there is no further bleeding, and Miss Bailey has bedrest for the next few weeks, I would hope that she can reach thirty-seven or thirty-eight weeks before the baby needs to be delivered.'

'I see.' Lanzo paused with his hand on the door to the ward. 'Will it be safe for her to fly to Italy by private jet, accompanied by a full medical team? I wish to take her to Rome to ensure that she rests properly, and I have arranged for her be cared for at a private hospital by one of Italy's top obstetricians.'

The doctor looked faintly startled, but nodded. 'Yes.

Ordinarily I would not allow her to fly, but with the arrangements you have organised for her care I think it should be okay. She can be discharged from here in the morning.'

'Then we will drive straight to the airport tomorrow,' Lanzo said in a determined voice.

Gina's eyes were swollen with crying, and at the totally unexpected sight of Lanzo striding down the ward more tears slipped silently down her cheeks.

'*Tesoro…*' His voice shook as he dropped down on the edge of the bed and drew her into his arms.

Gina did not know why he had come; she was still in shock from the nightmare events of the past few hours. All that mattered was that Lanzo was here. The horrible stilted phone calls of the past few weeks no longer seemed important as she clung to him and wept.

'I was so scared I was going to lose the baby. At first the doctor thought they would have to deliver early, but it's too soon—the baby is too small,' she sobbed.

'Shh, *cara*,' he soothed her, stroking her hair. 'You must stay calm for the baby's sake. Tomorrow I am taking you to Rome, so that you can be cared for by the best obstetrician in Italy.'

Gina eased away from him, suddenly conscious that she had cried all over the front of his no doubt exorbitantly expensive silk shirt. 'You don't have to do that. You don't need to be involved.' She fumbled for a tissue and blew her nose. 'My face puffs up like a frog when I cry,' she muttered.

Lanzo had never seen her cry like that before. To witness his strong, proud, beautiful Gina fall apart so utterly had evoked a terrible ache inside him, and his voice was gruff as he said, 'I've always liked frogs.'

Only Lanzo could make her smile when moments ago

she had been in the depths of despair. She needed his strength, but she dared not let him see how vulnerable she felt. 'I'll be okay. You don't need to take care of me out of some misplaced sense of duty,' she told him stiffly.

He winced, the familiar feeling of guilt clawing at his insides. 'Not because of duty,' he said. 'But because I want to.' She had told him that conceiving this baby had been a miracle—maybe her one chance to be a mother. 'I know how desperately you want this baby, *cara*, and I will do everything in my power to ensure you give birth safely,' he promised.

The last time Gina had been in Rome it had been stiflingly hot, but in February, although the sun was shining, the sky was a crisp, clear blue, and the temperature was twenty degrees lower than in the summer. Not that she had had much chance to walk outside. Her first two nights in the city had been spent at a private maternity hospital, where she had met the obstetrician who was to oversee her care.

'Strict bedrest, and I am afraid no sex,' Signor Bartolli had murmured when he'd come to her room to tell her that she could be discharged back to the apartment.

Agonisingly conscious of Lanzo's presence, Gina had blushed and carefully avoided his gaze, but she had felt a sharp pang of sadness that she was unlikely ever to make love with him again. He did not want to be a father to their child, and although he had surprised her by being involved now, her relationship with him would end once the baby was born.

'I don't think the doctor meant that I should spend every minute of the next few weeks actually in bed,' she'd argued the following day, after Lanzo had carried her through the apartment and deposited her as carefully as if she were made of spun glass onto the bed in one of the guestrooms.

'He meant precisely that—and so do I,' he said grimly, recognising the light of battle in her eyes. 'You are not to move out of this room, *cara*, and I plan to work from home to make sure you follow orders.'

'What about all your business trips?' Gina asked him.

'I have delegated them to my executives.' He sighed. 'Once again I am without a PA. Luisa has decided not to return to work after having her son,' he explained, 'and Raphaella only works part-time because she looks after her granddaughter two days a week.'

Granddaughter! So the exotic-sounding Raphaella was not some gorgeous young thing. The thought cheered Gina up no end. 'Why don't I fill in on the days Raphaella cares for her granddaughter?' she suggested. 'I can sit in bed with a laptop—that's hardly strenuous,' she pressed when Lanzo shook his head. 'I'm going to do as the doctor has told me—I'm certainly not going to do anything that might harm the baby—but I'll go mad if all I do is read magazines and watch daytime TV.'

'There *are* a couple of reports I need typed up,' Lanzo said slowly. 'I suppose it will be okay—as long as you promise to call it a day if you feel tired.'

For the first hour he trekked back and forth from his study to her room with various files, but eventually he brought his own laptop in and settled himself in the armchair near her bed. They worked in companionable silence.

'So, you're going ahead with the new restaurant in Toronto?' Gina commented, glancing down at the notes he had given her.

'Mmm—with a few changes to the menu. The chef wants to serve moose burgers.'

'*Really?*' She gave him a suspicious look when she saw his lips twitch. 'Are you kidding me?' she demanded, unable to hold back a smile when he grinned.

It was good to laugh with him again, she mused, tearing her eyes from the teasing warmth in his and staring at her computer screen. She had missed their friendship since they had argued on Christmas Day about his insistence that he did not want to be involved with their child.

The memory of his coldness when he had walked out of the house at Sandbanks caused her smile to fade, and she focused on the report in front of her.

With Lanzo and Daphne in constant attendance, Gina began to relax, and the trauma of being rushed into hospital in Poole, terrified that she was losing the baby, gradually faded. But two weeks later she woke in the early hours to find that she was bleeding heavily again. Her scream for Lanzo brought him hurtling into her room, and after that everything became a blur of paramedics, the wail of the ambulance siren, and nurses preparing her for surgery.

'I'm not due to give birth for another six weeks. Maybe the bleeding will stop, as it did before, and I can carry the baby for a little longer,' she begged the doctor when he told her she would have to undergo a Caesarean immediately.

But he shook his head, his face grave, and the last thing she remembered was Lanzo squeezing her hand and saying huskily, 'Everything will be all right, *cara*,' as she was wheeled into Theatre.

'Gina...'

Lanzo's voice sounded distant, and strangely muffled. Gina tried to open her eyes. Her lids felt as if they had been stuck down, but she finally managed to lift her lashes—and the first thing she saw was his tense face.

Her brain slammed into gear. *'The baby!'*

'A girl. You have a daughter, Gina.'

Even though her head was muzzy, she registered what he had said. *She* had a daughter—not we.

She licked her parched lips, feeling horribly sick from the anaesthetic. 'Is…is she all right?' He hesitated, and her heart stopped. *'Lanzo?'*

Lanzo heard the fear in her voice. 'She is fine,' he quickly sought to reassure her, 'but she is small…tiny…' Unbelievably tiny. The image of the little scrap of humanity he had seen briefly when a nurse had taken him to the special care unit was burned on his brain. 'She is in an incubator.' He hesitated once more, and then said gently, 'And on a ventilator to help her breathe, because her lungs are under-developed.'

Dear heaven. Gina swallowed, joy swiftly replaced by frantic worry. 'I want to see her.'

'You will soon, *cara*. But first the doctor is here to check you over.'

An hour later Lanzo wheeled Gina along to the special care baby unit.

'Why are there so many wires?' she asked shakily, blinking away the tears that blurred her eyes.

The moment she had first seen her little girl she had been overwhelmed with emotion. A tidal wave of love had swept through her, and now her hand shook as she touched the plastic side of the incubator. She longed to hold her child—but, as Lanzo had warned her, the baby was tiny. She seemed swamped by the nappy she was wearing, and surrounded by the tubes that were helping to keep her alive.

'But you're here, my angel,' Gina whispered, her eyes locked on her daughter's fragile body and mass of downy black hair. 'You are my little miracle, and I know you are going to make it.'

The paediatrician had talked of the potential problems that faced a premature baby born at thirty-four weeks and weighing under four pounds. Gina's face twisted when she recalled his warning of the high risk of infection and respiratory distress. The stark truth was that her daughter could not breathe without the ventilator that was giving her oxygen. In these early days her life would hang in the balance, but Gina refused to contemplate the worst.

She stared at her heartbreakingly delicate daughter, enclosed in the protective plastic bubble that was keeping her warm, and screwed up her eyes, determined not to allow the tears to fall. Crying wouldn't help, she reminded herself fiercely.

Lanzo could not bring himself to look at the child in the incubator. His one glance earlier had reinforced his belief that the skinny, wrinkled scrap had little chance of survival. He stood silently beside Gina, and the sight of her trying to hide her obvious distress evoked a dull ache inside him. He wanted to protect her from the pain of loss that he knew from bitter experience was almost unendurable.

'Try not to feel too deeply, *cara*,' he advised in a low tone. 'It would be better if you did not get too attached.'

Gina turned her head and looked at him blankly, unable to comprehend his words. Understanding slowly dawned, and she recoiled from him. Emotions swirled through her, the strongest of which was incandescent fury.

'*Don't get too attached?* She is my child—part of me—and part of you too, only you don't have the guts to face up to fatherhood,' she told him with withering scorn. 'Do you think that if I don't love her it will hurt less if she…?' She struggled with the words. 'If she doesn't make it? Is that what all this is about, Lanzo? I know your fiancée died, and your parents at the same time, and I don't doubt that must have been devastating for you—but you can't cut emotion from your life like it's a cancer that has to be removed.'

She took a shuddering breath. 'You are a coward. You might act the daredevil—taking part in dangerous sports like skydiving and powerboat racing—but you don't fear the risk to your personal safety. The real danger is to feel emotions—to put your heart on the line and take the chance of being hurt again, as you must have been when you lost your family. But that's a risk you're not prepared to take. Your baby is fighting for her life, and you refuse to *feel too deeply* because you don't want to deal with messy emotions like love and maybe…' her voice shook '…loss.'

Lanzo looked as though he had been carved from granite, but before he could respond a nurse pushed aside the curtain that had been drawn around them to allow some privacy, and announced that she had come to take Gina back to bed.

'I'm sure you must need some pain relief so soon after the Caesarean,' she said, smiling sympathetically when she saw Gina's drawn face. 'Then I will help you to express your milk, so that we can give it to your baby through the feeding tube until she is strong enough to feed from you herself.'

'I don't want to leave her,' Gina said thickly. She was determined to ignore the painful throb of her stitches and stay at her baby's side.

'You need to rest,' the nurse told her firmly. She smiled cheerfully at Lanzo. 'And her *papà* is here with her.'

The silence screamed with tension.

'He's just leaving,' Gina said dully, and did not glance at him again as the nurse pushed her wheelchair out of the SCBU.

CHAPTER TEN

LANZO raked a hand through his hair, shocked to realise that he was shaking. Gina's outburst had forced him to accept some bitter home truths, and he felt raw and exposed, as if she had peeled away layers of his skin.

He could not deny any of the accusations she had thrown at him, he acknowledged grimly. A coward? *Dio*, yes—she had been right to call him that when he had turned his back on her for most of her pregnancy and insisted that he did not want to be a father to their child.

He turned his head slowly towards the incubator, and felt his heart slam against his ribs when he found his tiny daughter gazing at him with big, deep blue eyes that were the image of her mother's. His breath caught in his throat as he took a jerky step closer to the incubator, and as he studied her perfect, miniature features the trembling in his limbs grew worse.

Utterly absorbed, he barely noticed the arrival of a nurse until she spoke. 'You can touch her,' she said softly. 'Put your hand through the window of the incubator—see?'

She was so tiny she would fit in his palm. Her skin was so fragile it was almost translucent. But she felt warm and soft, her chest rising and falling almost imperceptibly with each breath of life she took.

An indescribable sensation was unfurling deep inside

Lanzo. He gently stroked his daughter's tiny hand, and unbelievably she opened her minute fingers and curled them around his finger, her eyes still focused on his face as she clung to him.

Santa Madre, he was breaking apart. His throat was burning as if he had swallowed acid, and he tasted salt on his lips. Tears ran into his mouth.

'Here.' The nurse smiled gently and handed him a tissue. He couldn't stop the tears seeping from beneath his lashes, and he scrubbed his eyes with the tissue just as he had done when he had been a small boy who had grazed his knee and run to his mother for comfort.

He had cried after the fire—at the funerals of his parents and Cristina. But his grief had been agony, and he had learned to bury the pain deep inside him. For fifteen years he had locked his emotions away, but now, as he stared at his frail little daughter, it was as if a dam had burst and the feelings he had sought for so long to deny cascaded through him.

Gina had called the baby her miracle, but she was *his* miracle too—a tiny miracle who had unfrozen the ice around his heart. He did not have a choice of whether or not to love her, because love was seeping into every pore of his body—and he knew without even giving it conscious thought that he would give his life for his child.

'What do you think her chances are?' he asked the nurse gruffly. 'Do you think she will be okay?'

She nodded. 'I'm sure of it. She's a fighter, this little one. I've worked with premature babies for many years, and I sense she has a strong will.'

'She gets it from her mother,' Lanzo murmured, and sent up a fervent prayer of thanks that his daughter had inherited her mother's feisty nature.

* * *

Gina managed to contain her emotions until she was back in her private room and had obediently swallowed the pain-killers the nurse had handed her. But once she had been left alone to sleep the tears came—great, shuddering sobs that she tried to muffle by pressing her face into the pillow.

Her hormones were all over the place, she told herself when the storm finally passed, leaving her with a headache and hiccups. One of the things she had learned from life was that crying never solved anything, so she blew her nose and gingerly lay back on the pillows, wincing with the pain from her Caesarean wound. She needed to sleep and regain her strength so that she could care for her baby—because they were on their own now. No doubt Lanzo had left the hospital after the terrible things she had said to him. She had always known she was going to have to be a single mother, and for her baby's sake she had to stop feeling sorry for herself and get on with it.

It was early evening when she woke up, and she was horrified that she had slept for so long. The Caesarean had left her feeling as though she had been flattened by a truck, and she was relieved when a nurse told her it was too soon for her to try to walk yet, and wheeled her down to the special care baby unit.

She hadn't expected Lanzo to be there, sitting close to the incubator, his eyes never leaving the baby. He was still dressed in the jeans and black jumper he'd worn when she had been admitted to the hospital twelve hours earlier, and she had a strange feeling that he had been there all the time she had been asleep. He looked round when the nurse parked the wheelchair next to the incubator, an expression in his eyes that Gina could not define. She bit her lip, not knowing what to say to him, and he seemed to share her awkwardness for he quickly dropped his gaze to the book of baby names she had brought with her.

'I thought you had chosen a few possible names?' he murmured.

'None of them are right for her.' Gina's heart melted when her daughter gave a little yawn. It hadn't really sunk in until this moment that she was a mother, and a fierce wave of protectiveness swept through her. 'We can't keep on calling her "the baby".'

'What about naming her Andria?' Lanzo suggested. He hesitated, and then added softly, 'It means love—and joy.'

She threw him a sharp glance, but his green eyes were focused on his daughter and his thoughts were unfathomable. Hand trembling, she reached into the incubator and stroked the baby's silky black hair. 'Andria…it's perfect,' she whispered. Now it was her turn to hesitate. 'What was your mother's name?'

'Rosa.'

'Oh—that was Nonna Ginevra's second name.' Her eyes met his in a moment of silent agreement.

'Welcome to the world, Andria Rosa,' he said deeply, and to Gina's shock he put his hand into the incubator and placed it over hers.

Her heart jerked. She did not understand why he was here when he had been so insistent that he could not be a father, and especially after the things she had said to him, she thought ruefully. Dared she hope that he had had a change of heart? She was too afraid to ask, but a sense of peace settled over her as they sat in silence, two parents watching over their newborn daughter.

As the nurse had predicted, Andria Rosa was a fighter. She grew stronger day by day, and her cry became shriller. Gina did not mind. The sound of her daughter's voice filled her with utter joy and thankfulness for her miracle baby.

Every day brought a new landmark: the day Andria came off the ventilator, the first time Gina managed to walk to the SCBU rather than shuffle along in agony from her Caesarean scar, the first time she was able to hold her baby in her arms without all the tubes that had been keeping her alive, and breastfeeding her for the first time.

Gina recovered quickly, and was discharged ten days after the birth. Going back to the apartment without her baby was the one occasion when she wept, but Lanzo drove her to the hospital every day, and invariably stayed with her and their daughter in a private room.

'I know you must be busy with work.' Gina finally broached the subject she had been skirting around for days. He had been so adamant that his only role in their baby's life would be to provide financial support, and she was confused by his continued presence in Andria's life. 'You don't have to stick around,' she told him bluntly. 'You made it clear that you never wanted to be a father.'

A nerve flickered in his jaw, and he stared down at his daughter sleeping peacefully in his arms for long moments before he spoke. 'I honestly believed I did not want a child,' he admitted in a strained voice. 'You were right to accuse me of being a coward. I chose to live my life on my terms— selfishly only pleasing myself, refusing to allow myself to get too close to anyone—because it was easier that way, less complicated, and with no danger of ever being hurt.

'But then you conceived my baby, and for you it was the miracle you had believed would never happen. At first I was angry—determined that I would have no part in the child's life apart from to honour my financial responsibility. And then Andria was born.' He exhaled heavily. 'A tiny scrap who fought so hard to cling on to life. I feared that if you loved her you would be heartbroken if she lost her battle. I was trying to protect you,' he said, a plea for understanding in his voice as he met her startled gaze.

'You shamed me,' he told her roughly. 'You rounded on me like a tigress defending her cub, scornfully refusing the idea of withholding your love from our baby. You knew there was a danger she might not survive, but you loved her more—not less. You were not afraid to risk your heart, and I was humbled by your bravery, *cara*.'

There was so much more he needed to say to Gina, Lanzo acknowledged, so many things that were only now becoming clear to him—emotions that he could no longer deny. But after so many years of burying his feelings in the deepest, darkest reaches of his soul he was finding it hard to reveal what was in his heart.

She pushed her long hair back from her face, and his gut clenched as memories of running his fingers through the fall of chestnut silk assailed him. 'I'm not sure I understand what you're saying,' she mumbled, and Lanzo knew he could not blame her for sounding guarded after the way he had been.

'I'm saying that I want to be part of our daughter's life. I am her father, and I intend to devote myself to fulfilling that role—caring for her and protecting her.' His voice rasped in his throat as he thought briefly of how he had failed to protect Cristina. He pushed the thought away, determined to focus on the future. 'And most important of all loving her.'

Shock robbed Gina of words. She sensed Lanzo was waiting for her response, but she did not know what to say. Throughout her pregnancy she had prayed he would have a change of heart and accept his child, but now that he had she could see many problems ahead. Presumably access arrangements would have to be made, perhaps with solicitors involved, and decisions taken on where she and

Andria would live. Maybe Lanzo would want them to live in Italy, so that he could visit regularly, but she had expected to be a single mother and had planned to return to Poole so that she'd have the support of her family.

Andria stirred, and made the little snuffling sound that Gina instantly recognised as the sign she needed feeding. Her breasts felt heavy with milk, and she held out her arms when Lanzo brought the baby to her, maternal instinct taking over so that everything else faded from her mind but the intensity of love she felt for her daughter. One thing was certain: she would never agree to be parted from her child—which meant that if Lanzo wanted to be part of Andria's life he would have to be a continued presence in *her* life too.

The future was impossible to envisage, and so she stopped trying and focussed her attention exclusively on the little miracle in her arms.

They took their daughter home five weeks after her traumatic birth. Now weighing a healthy six pounds, Andria still seemed scarily tiny, but her demanding cry proved that there was now nothing at all wrong with her lungs. She was as pretty as a doll, with her blue eyes and mass of black hair, and Gina was utterly besotted with her.

Instead of taking the baby to the apartment, Lanzo explained that he had arranged for them to fly straight to the Villa di Sussurri in Positano.

'We'll have to buy a crib, and a pram,' Gina fretted, wishing that she had discussed living arrangements with Lanzo. She could not stay in any of his houses as a long-term guest. Andria needed a permanent home. But at the moment she did not even know whether she should plan to buy a house of her own in England or Italy.

'Everything has been taken care of,' Lanzo assured her.

'Daphne is already at the villa, and is desperate to meet the new addition to the family.'

But they weren't a family, Gina wanted to point out. Nothing was sorted out between them about how they were both going to be parents to Andria. And now a new problem had sprung up, she thought dismally as Lanzo lowered himself into the seat next to her on the jet, after checking that Andria was securely strapped into a special baby carrier. For the past weeks she had been enveloped in the haze of hormones that accompanied new motherhood, and her sudden acute awareness of Lanzo was unsettling.

If only the doctor at her postnatal check-up a few days ago had not mentioned that she could resume normal sexual activity whenever she felt ready. That very evening she had felt a tightening in the pit of her stomach when Lanzo had strolled bare-chested into the sitting room at the apartment, faded jeans hugging his lean hips and his hair still damp from his shower, and joined her on the sofa where she had been skimming through the TV channels. Then, as now, the scent of his aftershave had teased her senses, and she had been horrified to realise that she would be happy to 'resume normal sexual activity' right there on the sofa.

She had mumbled the excuse that she was tired and fled to her room, mortified by the amused gleam in his eyes that had warned her he had read her mind. Now, trapped in her seat as the jet sped down the runway, she tore her eyes from his handsome face and stared out of the window, every cell in her body tingling with awareness of his potent masculinity. He had said that he wanted his daughter, but had given no indication that he hoped to resume his relationship with *her*, Gina reminded herself. But, as she knew too well, he had a high sex-drive and it was likely he would soon take another mistress—perhaps he already had, she thought, jealousy searing her.

Lost in a labyrinth of dark thoughts, she gave a jolt when he reached out and closed his hand over hers. Her eyes flew to his, and for a second something flared in his green gaze that she could not define. His eyes narrowed; she recognised desire in their sultry gleam and hurriedly looked away, her heart thumping. Did he want them to be lovers once more? she wondered, her mind whirling. If so, how long would his desire for her last? And what would happen when he tired of her but still wanted to see his daughter?

The future loomed, an uncertain spectre, and she could not help thinking that it would have been easier if Lanzo had stuck to his original intention of turning his back on fatherhood—because that way she might have eventually got over him.

The white walls of the Villa di Sussurri gleamed in the spring sunshine, and although it was only April, pink roses were already blooming around the front door. Daphne greeted them with a beaming smile, her black eyes glowing as she cooed over the baby.

'I never thought I would see Lanzo look so happy,' she confided to Gina when Lanzo excused himself to make a brief business call. Gina was startled to see tears in the housekeeper's eyes. 'Cristina was the love of his life, and when she died his grief nearly destroyed him. But you and the *bambino*—you have brought joy to his heart once more.'

'You told me that she died in an accident. What happened to her?' Gina asked, seizing the chance to find out more about Lanzo's past.

But Daphne made no reply and hurried out of the room, leaving Gina with a host of unanswered questions. She wandered out to the hall and stared at the painting of the beautiful Italian girl Daphne said had been the love of Lanzo's life. The thought evoked a sharp pain inside her, a yearning for what could never be—for if Cristina had been his one true love, he was not likely ever to fall in love with her.

'Come and see the nursery,' Lanzo invited when he emerged from his study. He took Andria from her, and led the way upstairs and along the landing to a room that Gina knew was next to the master bedroom.

When she had stayed at the villa with him he had used this room as a dressing room, but now it had been transformed into a haven of powder-pink walls, carpet, and curtains, with a collection of fluffy toys on a shelf and a motif of cute white rabbits hopping around the room. Gina's eyes were drawn to the crib, with its exquisite white lace drapes. The nursery had been designed with loving care, but she did not understand why.

'Don't you like it?' he asked, when he saw her troubled face.

'It's beautiful—just the sort of nursery I would have planned,' she admitted, recalling how she had studied paint charts and debated colour schemes when she had been living at his house on Sandbanks. But she hadn't actually started to decorate a room for the baby because she had decided that she could not stay permanently in Lanzo's house—and she still felt that way now. 'It just seems such a waste to have gone to so much effort when Andria and I won't be staying at the villa for long.'

Lanzo placed his daughter tenderly in the crib and stood watching over her for a few moments, his heart aching with love for his child. The knowledge that he had been prepared to distance himself from her life chilled him to the bone. He had come so close to losing his precious little girl because he had been afraid to love her, and it was only thanks to Gina that he had seen sense.

He frowned as her words sank in. 'Of course you and Andria will be here, *cara*. I have decided that it will be better for her to grow up in Positano, rather than in Rome. The Amalfi Coast is so beautiful, and she can have a freedom here that would be impossible in the city.'

Gina felt a spurt of temper. Sometimes Lanzo could be so irritatingly arrogant and high-handed. 'What do you mean, *you've* decided? Surely the subject of where Andria will spend her childhood is something we should discuss together? We need to start planning how we can both be parents to her,' she said huskily. 'If you would prefer me to live with her in Italy rather than England then I am prepared to do that. I understand that you will want to visit her often—'

'I have no intention of *visiting* her,' Lanzo interrupted sharply. 'I told you—I want to be a proper father to Andria, which means living with her permanently as she grows up, having breakfast with her every morning, and tucking her into bed every night.' He paused and then dropped the bombshell. 'That is why I think the most sensible solution is for us to get married.'

Gina opened her mouth, but no words emerged. Lanzo's suggestion of marriage was utterly unexpected, and, although it was something she had long dreamed of, the reality did not evoke the slightest feeling of joy inside her. He had sounded so prosaic when he had offered his 'sensible solution', and those two words had shattered any faint hope she'd had that they could have any kind of a future together.

His eyes narrowed as he sensed her tension. 'We both want to be full-time parents to our daughter,' he reminded her.

'We don't have to get married to do that.'

'But it would be far better for Andria to be brought up by two parents who are committed to her and to each other.'

She could not deny it. She had always believed it was best for a child to grow up as part of a stable family unit. Marriage and children had been her holy grail. But not like this, she thought painfully. Not because it was a convenient solution to their living arrangements.

'I don't believe it would be a good idea to marry simply for Andria's sake,' she croaked, swallowing the lump that had formed in her throat.

'But it would not only be for that reason, *cara*.' Lanzo walked towards her, heat flaring inside him as he trailed his eyes slowly over her.

She had regained her figure remarkably quickly, and looked slim and sexy, her tight-fitting jeans moulding her bottom and her simple white tee clinging to her voluptuous curves. Many times when he had watched her feeding the baby he had felt a tug of desire that he had quickly stifled, but he could no longer fight his longing to bare her breasts and shape their swollen fullness with his hands.

'The chemistry still burns—for both of us,' he insisted softly, his eyes focusing on the faint tremor of her mouth. 'Did you think you could hide your awareness of me, when I know every inch of your body and recognise its every instinctive reaction to me? You cannot hide your desire for me, *cara*, any more than I can pretend that I am not burning up for you.'

His words, his tone, were beguiling. It would be so easy to give in and follow her heart rather than her head. But her head was urgently warning that he would break her heart, as he had done when she had been eighteen. She shook her head. 'That's just sex,' she muttered.

'It was always more than the slaking of a physical urge. We both know that,' he said deeply.

He had been aware from the beginning of their affair that she was the one woman who could make him break his promise to Cristina. Maybe it had started even further back than then, when she had been a plump, awkward eighteen-year-old, with a shy smile that had tugged on his heart?

Could she really believe that their sexual relationship meant something to him? Gina wondered bleakly. All the time she had been his PA he had never given any hint that he saw her as more than a temporary mistress.

'You wouldn't have considered marrying me if I hadn't had your baby,' she said stiffly.

There was no point in denying what they both knew to be the truth, Lanzo acknowledged grimly. But he was a different man now; Gina had changed him and made him see things differently.

'There is every reason to believe we could have a successful marriage. Added to our mutual desire to do the best for our daughter we share friendship, laughter…' he shrugged '…and, yes, good sex. What more is there?'

She swallowed the tears that clogged her throat. 'Well, if you don't know, there's not much point in me spelling it out. But the one thing missing from your list is presumably the most important reason why you asked Cristina to be your wife. Daphne said she was the love of your life,' she said, when he looked puzzled. '*Love* is the missing ingredient in our relationship, Lanzo, and that's the reason I won't marry you.'

He was staring at her intently, reading the emotions that she could not hide, and humiliation swept through her as understanding slowly dawned in his eyes. 'Gina?'

She could not bear to break down in front of him, but tears were filling her eyes, threatening to overspill.

'*Gina...*' he said again, his voice urgent.

She saw him take a step towards her, and with a choked cry she spun round and ran out of the nursery and down the stairs, her breath coming in agonising gasps as she paused before the portrait of his beautiful dead fiancée. *His one love.* The words pounded in her head, and, hearing his footsteps tearing down the stairs, she pulled open the front door and kept on running.

He found her in the walled garden, sitting by the pool, watching the goldfish darting between the lily pads. The realisation had hit her as she had fled down the drive that she could not run away from Lanzo because she had left Andria behind in the nursery, and nothing on earth would separate her from her baby.

Lanzo's footsteps slowed as he approached her. She could not bring herself to look at him, and after a few moments he came nearer and stared into the green depths of the pool.

The garden beds were ablaze with bright yellow narcissus, waving their heads in the breeze, and through the trees Gina glimpsed the dense blue of the sea. A curious sense of peace settled over her and she sighed. 'This is a beautiful place.'

'The garden was built over the site of my family home,' Lanzo told her, his voice harsh as he struggled to control the emotions storming inside him. 'The house was burned to the ground by a fire.' He paused. 'My parents and my fiancée were unable to escape.'

'Oh, God!' Gina felt sick. When Daphne had mentioned that Lanzo had lost his parents and fiancée in an accident, she had immediately thought of the narrow, winding road along the Amalfi Coast and imagined that they had been involved in a car crash. Not that it would have been any better, she thought with a shiver. But to be trapped in a burning building was truly horrific. 'What happened?' she whispered.

He turned to face her, and she caught her breath at the raw pain in his eyes. She had believed once that he was hollow inside, incapable of feeling the normal range of emotions other human beings felt. But she saw now she had been wrong.

'There was a storm one night and the house was struck by lightning. It was an old house, built in the seventeenth century, and the dry timbers in the roof caught alight instantly. Within minutes flames had engulfed the top floors where my parents slept.' A nerve jumped in Lanzo's cheek. 'My mother and father both struggled with the stairs. I had nagged them to move to a bedroom on one of the lower floors, but my mother loved the view from the top of the house. They didn't stand a chance,' he said heavily. 'The fire crew told me later that the flames had been fanned by high winds and the house went up like tinder.'

'So you weren't you here when the fire happened?' Gina murmured.

'No.' His voice rasped in his throat. 'And I have never forgiven myself. I should have been here. Cristina had begged me not to go to Sweden for a business meeting.' He closed his eyes briefly, the memories still hurting even though so many years had passed. 'She had just told me that she was pregnant,' he revealed huskily.

His mouth twisted when Gina could not restrain a gasp of shock. 'I'm ashamed to say that I reacted badly. We were both very young, and had agreed not to start a family for several years so that I could concentrate on preparing to take over the running of Di Cosimo Holdings when my father retired. I didn't feel ready to be a father,' he admitted. 'I stormed out like a spoiled child. But while I was away my common sense returned. I knew we would manage, knew that I would love our child, and I was impatient to get back to Positano to reassure Cristina that I was pleased about the baby.' His jaw clenched. 'But my meeting overran, I missed my flight, and I had to wait and catch the first flight home the next morning—by which time it was too late to tell Cristina anything,' he said grimly.

'You couldn't have known what would happen,' Gina said gently. 'You can't blame yourself.'

His jaw tightened. 'But I do. I knew nothing about the fire until I arrived at Naples Airport and was met by Cristina's father. When he broke the news that she and my parents were gone I knew that it was my fault. I could have saved them,' he insisted harshly when Gina shook her head. 'If only I hadn't gone away I would have got them out of the house—even if I'd had to carry both my parents down the stairs.'

Gina shivered again as she pictured the terrible scene. 'Was Cristina's room at the top of the house too?' She could understand why Lanzo's elderly parents had been trapped, but the portrait of Cristina showed that she had been young and able-bodied, so why hadn't she escaped?

'She was asleep in my room, on the floor below my parents. Daphne was in the staff quarters on the ground floor and was awoken by the sound of the fire alarm. She knew Cristina would not have heard it, and she tried desperately to reach her, but the stairs were already alight and the smoke was too thick.' Lanzo sighed. 'Poor Daphne has never forgiven herself for escaping and leaving the others. She cannot bear to speak of the events of that night.'

'But—*why* didn't Cristina hear the alarm? *Why* didn't she try to get out?'

He let out a ragged breath. 'She was profoundly deaf.

She'd had meningitis as a child, and lost her hearing as a result of the illness.'

'Oh, Lanzo.' Gina stood up and walked over to him. 'I'm so sorry.' The words sounded banal. Driven by an instinctive need to comfort him, she wrapped her arms around his rigid body. For a moment he did not move, and then he lifted his hand and threaded his fingers through her hair.

'Cristina was my childhood friend,' he explained quietly. 'We grew up together and I had always taken care of her. I was looking forward to doing so for the rest of my life. Sometimes she used to get upset about her deafness, and worry that that I would want to be with someone from the hearing world, but I promised her that I would never love another woman, only her. If I had not gone off in a temper and left her she would not have died,' he said raggedly. 'I failed to take care of her and the child she had just conceived, but standing at her graveside I repeated the promise I had made to her that I would never replace her in my heart.'

Gina understood, she truly did, but even though she now knew why he could never love her it did not make her heartache any less, she thought sadly. She guessed that Lanzo had never grieved properly for the people he loved, but had buried his pain deep inside him. She understood why he had refused to risk his emotions. It must have been hard for him to open his heart to his baby daughter, but he loved Andria and wanted to be her father.

After all he had suffered, how could she deny him his daughter? But how could she marry him when she knew that his heart belonged irrevocably to the girl whose beautiful smile still greeted him in the hallway of his home? Feeling suddenly awkward at the way she was clinging to him, she loosened her arms and took a step backwards.

'You didn't fail Cristina. Fate was cruel that night, but

you could not have changed it, and I don't think that the woman whose love for you shines from her face in that painting would have wanted you to spend the rest of your life consumed with guilt.' Gina blinked back the tears that blurred her eyes. 'I think Cristina would have wanted you to find happiness again,' she said huskily.

She half expected Lanzo to deny that he could ever be happy again, and she was startled when he closed the gap between them and drew her against his chest, holding her so close that she could feel the hard thud of his heart.

'How wise you are, *cara mia*,' he said gently. 'Whereas I am a fool who has taken far too long to accept what I know in my heart is true. I know that Cristina would not have wanted me to grieve for ever, but I used the promise I made at her grave as a shield. I never again wanted to suffer the pain I felt after the fire, so I clung to that promise and used it as an excuse for why I could not fall in love.'

He eased back from her a little and stared into her face, the expression in his eyes causing Gina's heart to miss a beat.

'I can't hide from the truth any more, or deny how I feel about you any longer,' he said, his deep voice shaking with emotion. 'I love you, Gina, with all my heart and soul and everything that I am.'

She stared back at him wordlessly, scared to believe it could be true. She had seen him look at Andria with tender adoration blazing in his eyes, and had wished with all her heart that he could look at her the same way. It seemed that her heart had been granted its dearest wish, but her vision was blurred with tears and she was afraid to accept what her eyes were telling her. She thought about his broken promise and bit her lip.

'Even if it's true, you can't feel happy about…loving

me if you feel guilty that you have betrayed Cristina,' she whispered.

Lanzo smiled and tilted her face to his, wiping away the tears that slipped down her cheeks with unsteady fingers. 'It *is* true, and loving you makes me the happiest man in the world, *tesoro mio.*'

He glanced around the garden that he had created as a memorial to the woman who had been his first love. He would always have special memories of Cristina, but Gina had taught him to love again. She had given him his precious daughter, and a future that he hoped to share with her for the rest of his life. His heart overflowed with his love for her.

'You are my life, Gina,' he murmured. 'You and Andria are my reasons for living, and I will no longer risk my life by taking part in dangerous sports.'

She managed a wobbly smile, joy unfurling tentatively inside her. 'You mean you're giving up skydiving and powerboat racing?' It was difficult to believe that the daredevil playboy would be content with a quiet life. 'How will you satisfy your need for excitement?' she asked doubtfully.

'You are all the adrenalin rush I need, *cara,*' he murmured, his green gaze glinting as he pulled her against him and watched her eyes widen when she felt the hard ridge of his arousal.

'Lanzo…' His mouth was a sensual temptation she had been denied for too long, and a tremor ran through her when he brushed his lips over hers in a gentle kiss that tugged on her heart. She wanted more—needed the fierce passion that was so intrinsic to their relationship—and her mouth quivered when he broke the kiss and lifted his head.

'There is something you can do for me. Marry me— please, *amore*. Not for Andria's sake,' he said urgently as she bit her lip, 'or for any reason other than that you are the love of my life and I want to spend my life making you happy.' He lightly touched the scar on her neck. 'You deserve to be happy, Gina, and I promise I will never do anything to hurt you.'

He was nothing like her first husband. She had always known that. 'You did hurt me once,' she admitted softly. 'I fell in love with you when I was eighteen and you broke my heart. And then, to add insult to injury, you went away and forgot about me.'

He shook his head. 'I never forgot you. Over the years I was drawn back to Poole, although I did not acknowledge that it was because I was looking for the girl with a shy smile. And then, when we finally met again, I did not realise at first that the beautiful, elegant Ginevra Bailey was *my* Gina.'

'*Your* Gina?' she questioned, startled by the depth of emotion in his voice.

He nodded, suddenly sombre. 'I started to fall in love with you ten years ago, but when I realised that you were a threat to my heart I ran for the hills. I was afraid to love you,' he admitted. 'But I am not afraid any more.'

He stroked his fingers through her long hair and Gina was puzzled by the sudden uncertainty in his eyes.

'I wouldn't mind knowing how the girl who was in love with me ten years ago feels about me now,' he said roughly.

She smiled then, although tears were not far away. Maybe dreams really could come true. 'Oh, she still loves you. Deep in her heart she never stopped,' she told him softly.

He swallowed, welcoming the tidal wave of emotion that swept through him rather than trying to fight it as he had for so long. 'And will you be my wife, *amore mio*, and stay with me for ever?'

'I will.' It was a promise from her heart.

He kissed her with exquisite tenderness, and then, as passion overwhelmed them, with a hunger that she shared. His hands roamed feverishly over her slender body as he crushed her lips beneath his, and he slid his tongue into her mouth, deepening the kiss until she was trembling—or was it him?

She smiled at his obvious pleasure when he drew her tee shirt over her head and unclipped her bra, so that her breasts spilled into his hands. He tugged her jeans over her hips and knelt to draw her knickers down, before slipping his hand between her thighs and caressing her with infinite care until she gasped and squirmed and begged him to make love to her.

'With my body and my heart,' he assured her as he stripped off his own clothes and drew her down onto the camomile lawn that enveloped them in its sweet fragrance.

He entered her slowly, afraid that he would hurt her when they had not made love for months, but she welcomed him eagerly into her and lifted her hips to meet each gentle thrust, until he could not hold back and took them both swiftly to the pinnacle of pleasure.

'*Ti amo*, Gina, always and for ever,' he groaned as they climaxed together and fell back down to earth safe in each other's arms.

She captured his face in her hands and pressed her lips against his damp lashes. It had been a long journey for both of them, but finally they had found each other—and a love that would last for eternity.

'Always and for ever, my love,' she agreed.

EPILOGUE

THEY were married a month later, in the church in Positano. All of Gina's family flew out for the wedding, and the ceremony was a joyous affair, full of love and laughter. The bride wore a simple ivory silk gown and pink roses in her hair, and the groom looked impossibly handsome in a dark grey suit. The tender smile on his face when he kissed his new wife caused Daphne to burst into tears, but the smallest guest stole the day—for it was also Andria Rosa's christening. The baby looked angelic, in a froth of white lace, and smiled and gurgled happily unless her father tried to put her down, when she squawked indignantly.

'Our daughter might be small, but she is very determined,' Lanzo murmured when he placed Andria in her mother's arms and she immediately snuggled into Gina's neck. 'I wonder where she gets it from?' he added dryly.

They held a reception in the walled garden, and later, when all the guests had departed and Daphne had taken charge of Andria, Lanzo swept Gina into his arms and carried her into the villa.

'Where is the painting of Cristina?' she asked, noticing immediately the space on the wall where the portrait had hung.

'I've taken it down and put it away. You are my wife, *cara*. The Villa di Sussurri is your home, and I did not think you would want to have a reminder of my past on display.'

Lanzo's green eyes were no longer shadowed, Gina noticed, but clear and blazing with emotion as he stared down at her. She had not been his first love, but she had no doubt now that he loved her with all his heart—just as she loved him.

'Cristina was a special person in your life, and I know you will never forget her—nor would I want you to,' she told him softly. 'She is part of your past, and she belongs here. Put the painting back, Lanzo.'

'Have I told you how much I love you, Signora di Cosimo?' Lanzo said deeply as he carried her up the stairs to their bedroom.

Her smile stole his breath. 'Many times. But you can tell me again—and show me,' she invited huskily when he laid her on the bed.

'I intend to, *cara*,' he promised. 'For the rest of my life.'

Harlequin *Presents*

Coming Next Month

from **Harlequin Presents® EXTRA.** Available July 12, 2011

Coming Next Month

from **Harlequin Presents®.** Available July 26, 2011

Visit www.HarlequinInsideRomance.com
for more information on upcoming titles!

REQUEST YOUR FREE BOOKS!

♦Harlequin *Presents*

PASSION
GUARANTEED
SEDUCTION

2 FREE NOVELS PLUS
2 FREE GIFTS!

YES! Please send me 2 FREE Harlequin Presents® novels and my 2 FREE gifts (gifts are worth about $10). After receiving them, if I don't wish to receive any more books, I can return the shipping statement marked "cancel." If I don't cancel, I will receive 6 brand-new novels every month and be billed just $4.05 per book in the U.S. or $4.74 per book in Canada. That's a saving of at least 15% off the cover price! It's quite a bargain! Shipping and handling is just 50¢ per book in the U.S. and 75¢ per book in Canada.* I understand that accepting the 2 free books and gifts places me under no obligation to buy anything. I can always return a shipment and cancel at any time. Even if I never buy another book, the two free books and gifts are mine to keep forever.

106/306 HDN FC55

Name _____ (PLEASE PRINT) _____

Address _____ Apt. # _____

City _____ State/Prov. _____ Zip/Postal Code _____

Signature (if under 18, a parent or guardian must sign) _____

Mail to the **Reader Service:**
IN U.S.A.: P.O. Box 1867, Buffalo, NY 14240-1867
IN CANADA: P.O. Box 609, Fort Erie, Ontario L2A 5X3

Not valid for current subscribers to Harlequin Presents books.

**Are you a current subscriber to Harlequin Presents books
and want to receive the larger-print edition?
Call 1-800-873-8635 or visit www.ReaderService.com.**

* Terms and prices subject to change without notice. Prices do not include applicable taxes. Sales tax applicable in N.Y. Canadian residents will be charged applicable taxes. Offer not valid in Quebec. This offer is limited to one order per household. All orders subject to credit approval. Credit or debit balances in a customer's account(s) may be offset by any other outstanding balance owed by or to the customer. Please allow 4 to 6 weeks for delivery. Offer available while quantities last.

Your Privacy—The Reader Service is committed to protecting your privacy. Our Privacy Policy is available online at www.ReaderService.com or upon request from the Reader Service.

We make a portion of our mailing list available to reputable third parties that offer products we believe may interest you. If you prefer that we not exchange your name with third parties, or if you wish to clarify or modify your communication preferences, please visit us at www.ReaderService.com/consumerchoice or write to us at Reader Service Preference Service, P.O. Box 9062, Buffalo, NY 14269. Include your complete name and address.

HP11

*Once bitten, twice shy. That's Gabby Wade's motto—
especially when it comes to Adamson men.
And the moment she meets Jon Adamson her theory
is confirmed. But with each encounter a little something
sparks between them, making her wonder if she's been
too hasty to dismiss this one!*

*Enjoy this sneak peek from ONE GOOD REASON
by Sarah Mayberry, available August 2011
from Harlequin® Superromance®.*

Gabby Wade's heartbeat thumped in her ears as she marched
to her office. She wanted to pretend it was because of her
brisk pace returning from the file room, but she wasn't that
good a liar.

Her heart was beating like a tom-tom because Jon Adamson had touched her. In a very male, very possessive way.
She could still feel the heat of his big hand burning through
the seat of her khakis as he'd steadied her on the ladder.

It had taken every ounce of self-control to tell him to
unhand her. What she'd really wanted was to grab him by
his shirt and, well, explore all those urges his touch had
instantly brought to life.

While she might not like him, she was wise enough to
understand that it wasn't always about liking the other person. Sometimes it was about pure animal attraction.

Refusing to think about it, she turned to work. When
she'd typed in the wrong figures three times, Gabby admitted she was too tired and too distracted. Time to call it a
day.

As she was leaving, she spied Jon at his workbench in
the shop. His head was propped on his hand as he studied
blueprints. It wasn't until she got closer that she saw his

eyes were shut.

He looked oddly boyish. There was something innocent and unguarded in his expression. She felt a weakening in her resistance to him.

"Jon." She put her hand on his shoulder, intending to shake him awake. Instead, it rested there like a caress.

His eyes snapped open.

"You were asleep."

"No, I was, uh, visualizing something on this design." He gestured to the blueprint in front of him then rubbed his eyes.

That gesture dealt a bigger blow to her resistance. She realized it wasn't only animal attraction pulling them together. She took a step backward as if to get away from the knowledge.

She cleared her throat. "I'm heading off now."

He gave her a smile, and she could see his exhaustion.

"Yeah, I should, too." He stood and stretched. The hem of his T-shirt rose as he arched his back and she caught a flash of hard male belly. She looked away, but it was too late. Her mind had committed the image to permanent memory.

And suddenly she knew, for good or bad, she'd never look at Jon the same way again.

Find out what happens next in ONE GOOD REASON, available August 2011 from Harlequin® Superromance®!

Celebrating

Blaze **10** *years of*
red-hot reads

Featuring a special August author lineup of
six fan-favorite authors who have written
for Blaze™ from the beginning!

The Original Sexy Six:

Vicki Lewis Thompson
Tori Carrington
Kimberly Raye
Debbi Rawlins
Julie Leto
Jo Leigh

Pick up all six Blaze™
Special Collectors' Edition titles!

August 2011

Plus visit
HarlequinInsideRomance.com
and click on the Series Excitement Tab
for exclusive Blaze™ 10th Anniversary content!

USA TODAY *bestselling author*

Lynne Graham

introduces her new Epic Duet

THE VOLAKIS VOW
A marriage made of secrets...

Tally Spencer, an ordinary girl with no experience of relationships... Sander Volakis, an impossibly rich and handsome Greek entrepreneur. Sander is expecting to love her and leave her, but for Tally this is love at first sight. Little does he know that Tally is expecting his baby...and blackmailing him to marry her!

PART ONE:
THE MARRIAGE BETRAYAL
Available August 2011

PART TWO:
BRIDE FOR REAL
Available September 2011

Available only from Harlequin Presents®.